MAXI

Witchcraft in the twentieth century? A computer controlled demon? Maxim Gunn didn't believe it either until his old enemy, Wanda Liszt, miraculously returned from the dead with another insane plan to control the world.

Ambushes, a terrible booby trapped tomb, a demonic attack by the fiend Wanda controls, keep Gunn on his toes until, with a little help from the giant Swedish archeologist, Torquil Tornquist, the earthshaking finale is reached.

MAXIM GUNN

AND

THE DEMON PLAN

This book is entirely fiction. Any resemblance to actual people, living or dead, is purely coincidental

MAXIM GUNN AND THE DEMON PLAN

Published by:

TAURUS PUBLISHING
55-41 Falconer Drive, Mississauga
Ontario, Canada, L5N 1B3

CANADIAN CATALOGUING IN PUBLICATION DATA

Boving, Nicholas 1939 -
Maxim Gunn and The Demon Plan

"A Maxim Gunn Adventure"
ISBN 1-896448-01-1

1. Title

PS 8553.08983M39 1997 C813' .54 C97-931179-9
PR9199.3.B68M39 1997

A MAXIM GUNN ADVENTURE

"Whatever happens, we have got
Maxim Gunn, and they have not"

I would like to thank my wife, Joan, for her support, her patience and, above all, determination to get it right.

Also a special thanks to Linda Kwan, who proof read and copyedited the original manuscript. I dedicate this to them.

Nicholas Boving

CHAPTER ONE

In total silence the watcher peered through the grill at the end of the air duct, into the well lit room below, and found it frightening. It was a contrary mixture of hard, practical technology in the shape of a bank of computers, the tape reels whirring and clicking as they sorted information, the display consoles flickering eerily in the subdued light, and the weird, cabalistic signs inlaid into the cold, tiled floor, and worked into silk hangings on the otherwise bare walls.

At the control console sat a man, some sixty years of age to judge by his almost white hair, busily entering instructions into the programme, and from time to time checking his progress against a thick file of printouts.

The watcher remained motionless, hardly daring to breathe. The proof, the culmination of months of painstaking work and tracking had led him to where he was now, and just a few more minutes would give him the proof he needed.

For a moment he closed his eyes and lowered his head. God, how tired he was. And then he pulled himself together. One final effort and he'd be able to get out, back to base and report; to hand these people over to those more properly equipped to deal with them.

The man at the console finally finished his work, typed a last group of symbols and closed the file. He glanced at his watch and got up, walked to the door and went out.

The watcher waited until he was sure no-one was coming back, and then, grasping the grill firmly, he pushed it off its clips and drew it back into the duct. Then he eased himself forward, wriggled out of the opening and dropped quietly to the floor.

He crouched, listening intently, moved towards the glass windowed double doors at the far end and looked through.

The room was small, not more than eight feet square, and completely featureless apart from a chrome plated chair standing in the centre. Sitting rigidly upright and strapped into the chair was a man, his face expressionless. The eyes were wide open and had the vacant, staring look of a man who could no longer call his mind his own.

The watcher instinctively started to push the doors, and then he dropped his arms and bowed his head. He knew there was nothing he could do. Instead, he took a camera out of the bag he was carrying and began to take a series of shots.

So engrossed was he in taking the shots that he didn't hear the door of the computer room open, nor the silent figure which crept across the tiled floor behind him. All he was briefly aware of was a crashing blow on the back of the head and a scrambled mess of flashing lights as he lost consciousness.

Slowly consciousness returned, and with it a painfully throbbing head and a dry mouth. As his eyes focused he tried to move and found himself bound hand and foot in a sitting position, and realized with a cold chill of horror that it was now he who was strapped to the chrome plated chair.

He straightened and lifted his head, staring with dulled eyes at the double doors, and waited.

It seemed like hours, but was probably no more than a few minutes before he heard footsteps and voices in the computer room, and then the double doors opened.

Two people came into the room. One was a man; tall

and imposing with a fine head of white hair, who might have been a great artist or musician. He looked coldly at the man in the chair and turned to his companion, a woman of dark and startling beauty. The prisoner felt his skin crawl with fear.

The woman spoke, her voice low and musical, but with the chill of Arctic ice.

`No doubt you have some idea of the work we are carrying out, Mr Henderson,' she said. `Oh yes, I know your name. If so, you know too much. We must therefore ensure that your knowledge goes no further.'

Henderson heard the death sentence, and against all odds became calm. When there is no hope, then emotion dies. But at least he had got one report away. Whether it would reach its intended destination was another matter.

The woman went on. `You will not die in vain, and you will find out the truth in the process. Good-bye, Mr Henderson.' The doors swung silently behind her as she left.

CHAPTER TWO

The sunlight flickered on the ripples of the chalk stream as Maxim Gunn expertly made his cast with the fly rod. The gossamer line settled on the water like a strand of hair, and the fly drifted exactly over the spot where he was almost sure the old trout lurked. There was a sluggish swirl as a dark shape nosed curiously upwards and then sank back. Gunn slowly gathered the line and prepared to make another cast. He'd get it today; he could feel it in his bones.

Maxim Gunn was at peace, with himself and the world. He called no man master since leaving the dirty, dangerous and at times downright boring life he had known as an agent for one of his country's covert organizations. That life was gone, and he blessed his decision to rid himself of it. In its place he had friends, his house in London, freedom to do as he pleased - and peace.

Unaccountably he felt a twinge of irritation, and badly misjudged the next cast, snagging his line in a low hanging branch of a willow which hung over the water.

For a few moments he considered the problem, and then with a quick movement, snapped the filament, leaving the fly, a forlorn reminder that the old trout had chosen his lair well. Gunn packed his rod, all desire to capture the old beast suddenly gone. It had lived this long through hard earned cunning. He would let it alone, and besides, the only way to retrieve the fly involved a wetting.

As he put his rod and creel in the trunk of the Lagonda, he became aware of an uneasiness that spoiled the beauty of the late evening. Midges danced in the warm air, a lark sang as if its heart was bursting with joy, and a couple of mallards came in for foot-splayed landings a hundred yards upstream from the pool where the old trout lurked. It was all so peaceful, so perfect, a summer evening at its picture book best. He ought to be joining the lark and shouting for sheer joy. But he wasn't. That final miscast had twanged a chord somewhere in his inner being. It was such a little thing, and yet it upset him in a way he couldn't put a finger on.

He slammed the trunk shut and got into the car, frowning as he started the motor. Dammit, this was supposed to be a holiday; nothing was supposed to be wrong. And yet something was.

As he drove the big car down the lane to the road that would take him back to his hotel, an uneasy suspicion rose unbidden in his mind. Maybe it was all too perfect. Maybe life was too peaceful. Maybe the sight of the old trout rising warily, rejecting his fly and then disappearing to fight another day was meant as some kind of message. Had he risen and taken the lure of ease and good living, when what his being really needed was challenge and action.

He reached the road, and in a moment of anger, slammed his foot to the floor. The V8 motor roared like a beast unleashed, and minutes later he skidded to a stop on the gravelled drive in front of the Tudor building, a relic of the past, long since converted to cater to the comforts of fishermen.

Gunn got out, mildly ashamed at his childish action, walked quickly through the open doors and made for the bar, where he ordered a malt whisky before going to his room to shower and change for dinner.

As he entered the room the phone rang. It was the manager.

`Mr Gunn. Sorry to disturb you, but there was a call for you while you were out.'

`Oh yes,' Gunn replied, puzzled. He had given strict orders not to be contacted by anyone unless it was an emergency. `Did the person leave a message?'

`Yes, Sir. It was a Miss Anders. The number she gave was ..'

`I know it,' Gunn cut in. `Thank you.'

`Thank you, Mr Gunn. Will you be dining tonight?'

`Yes, I will. I'll be down shortly.'

`Shall we prepare your catch, Sir?' asked the manager.

`Hard to prepare nothing,' replied Gunn. `I think I'll have one of yours instead.'

He hung up, quickly stripped and went into the bathroom in a queer mixture of resentment and excitement. What the devil did Polly Anders want? he thought. And then he got under the shower, and found himself whistling lightheartedly as if a weight had suddenly been lifted from his mind.

The fishing may not have been a success, but the dinner was. He had trout in lemon parsley butter, followed by local strawberries and cream, and washed it down with a good Australian hock to which he had become rather partial. Then he took his coffee into the lounge, ordered a brandy and asked for a telephone. He might as well find out what Polly wanted.

As he waited he thought about the girl he was soon to speak with, and the possible reasons for her call.

Polly Anders was nominally secretary to his old Chief at the agency where he used to work. Secretary in so far as she did work for him that was too sensitive to be given to anyone else, good though they might be; and nominally in that she was also a superbly competent undercover agent in her own right.

At first glance, Polly gave the impression of golden hair, cornflower blue eyes and a slightly vacuous expression. The overall look was that of the classic dumb blond. Gunn, and everyone else at the agency knew better. Behind that breathless, low I.Q. front was a brain like a computer, nerves of steel, and a courage that was little short of awe inspiring. Many people had been fooled by her, and some had lived to regret it. Others simply hadn't lived.

The reason for her call was conjecture, and Gunn wasn't in the habit of conjecturing in the absence of facts.

His brandy and the phone arrived simultaneously, and moments later he was connected to a highly classified number not far from the British Museum in London. He identified himself, heard the click and hum as a recorder went into operation, and then Polly Anders answered.

`You took your time,' she said, accusingly.

`As a gentleman of leisure I'm entitled to,' replied Gunn, smoothly.

Polly made an unladylike noise. `Vileman wants to see you.'

Gunn felt his pulse quicken by a couple of beats a minute.

`I'm not sure I want to see him.'

`It's important, Maxim.'

`Then he knows where to find me, doesn't he. Incidentally, how did you know I was here?'

Polly laughed and put on a stage Jewish accent. `Not a sparrow falls, my dear.'

Gunn grunted noncommittally. `I'm not sure I like that. We had an agreement when I left.'

Polly laughed. `Since when did that stop the Chief? Are you going to see him?'

`I'll see him. What's it all about, anyway?'

`Not over the phone. When can you be here?'

`I'm not going to be anywhere, except here,' said Gunn.

`But you said ..'

`I said I'd see him, and it seems he knows where to find me.'

`Maxim, I think that's most unreasonable.'

`Why? He doesn't own me. I don't work for him any more. If he wants me he can come to me. And besides, I'm on holiday.'

`One day won't make much difference. He'd appreciate it. Maxim, I think he's worried.'

`Good,' replied Gunn, with feeling.

Polly coughed delicately. `I'll buy you lunch.'

The game had gone on long enough. Gunn knew he had been hooked the moment he heard her voice. Vileman wouldn't want to see him unless there was something pretty big in the wind, and unless there was no-one else he could turn to. He mentioned a very expensive restaurant.

`O.K.' said Polly, with a sigh. `The things I do for England. When can you be here?'

`Give me time to pack my bag.' He glanced at his watch. `Say two and a half hours from now.'

Fifteen minutes later he threw his battered leather hold-all onto the back seat of the Lagonda and got behind the wheel. He touched the starter and the big engine throbbed into life. For a moment he studied the instruments, their blue green glow lighting his lean, hard face, and then, satisfied that all was well, engaged drive and took off. Two and a half hours hard driving would take him to the dingy office in London. He settled down to concentrate on the road ahead.

The sun finally dipped below the horizon as he was crossing Salisbury Plain. The car's headlights lanced through the gathering darkness like twin gun barrels and he flashed past a thundering truck heading for the city markets as if it had been standing still. Gunn had a supreme disregard for the speed laws of any country, but as a driver who could hold his own with the best in the world, he was well within his limits as the needle hovered around the hundred mile an hour mark. Lightning flickered on the hills to his left, somewhere in the region of Stonehenge; it was a night for a wild ride and he felt a crawl of excitement in the pit of his stomach.

Shortly after nine o'clock he was approaching the western suburbs of London and slowed as the traffic thickened, and it was at a sedate pace that he passed through the West End and turned up Shaftesbury Avenue. Minutes later he rounded St Giles Circus, passed the imposing bulk of the British Museum on his left and took a quick right turn.

The clocks were just striking ten as he pulled up outside the uninspiring grey building that housed the organization for which he used to work. He got out, locked the car and went up the steps and through the grimy double glass doors.

To the casual passer-by, the building purported to house a firm specializing in the restoration of paintings, a dealer in rare books and a Methodist Missionary Society, none of which existed. Inquiries would be met at the front desk by polite regrets to the effect that there was either no-one at home, or the company concerned had just filed for bankruptcy. Either way, that was as far as they would have got. Any attempt to press the issue would have meant getting past ex-SAS Sergeant `Earthquake' Magoon or his opposite number, an ex-Marine by the name of O'Rourke, both very tough customers.

The lobby was in keeping with the exterior of the building. Worn linoleum covered the floor, and peeling paint of a particularly unappetizing green coated the walls to shoulder height. Above that it changed to a dirty off-white before melding with the smoke blackened ceiling. Gunn walked to a glass fronted porter's booth stuck in a corner by an antique elevator. The man in the booth looked up quickly.

`Evening, Sergeant,' said Gunn. `A bit late aren't you?'

Sergeant Magoon folded his copy of the *Evening Standard* and smiled.

`Never off duty, Sir. You know how it is.'

`Don't remind me. And how have you been keeping?'

`Very well, Sir. And all the better for seeing you.'

`It seems I can't keep away from the place, Sergeant.'

`Yes, Sir. Miss Anders told me you'd be coming.'

`The Chief wants ...'

`What the Chief wants ..' began Magoon, with feeling.

`Now, now,' laughed Gunn.

`Yes, Sir. You're to go straight up.'

Gunn raised an eyebrow. ` No passes, no search?'

Magoon shook his head. `No Sir. Not this time. Anyway, you don't have a pass anymore.'

Gunn grinned. `You know, that makes me feel good.'

Magoon grunted. `You know the way, Sir.'

Gunn nodded, gave him a sketchy salute and made for the elevator.

The offices of the agency were in total contrast to the seedy atmosphere of the entrance foyer. No expense had been spared in the interests of efficiency and proper working conditions. Vileman may not have been liked by the Establishment, but he got what he wanted, and had gone to considerable trouble to ensure that the place where his people worked was conducive to their best efforts. The place was not sound proofed, but sound deadened, and as Gunn left the elevator he was immediately struck once again by the muted hum of efficiency. There were no loud noises, no clashing colours, nothing to take the eye from the job in hand; nothing jarred in any way whatsoever. His remarks to Magoon had not referred to the decor.

Maxim Gunn moved quietly into the third floor offices and leaned against a door jamb, one eyebrow raised and a quizzical smile on his lips, and for the hundredth time wondered how anyone who gave the appearance of being as mildly moronic as she did, could in reality be so smart.

`How do you manage it?' he asked.

Polly turned at the sound of his voice, and flashed him a bright eyed smile. `Manage what?'

`Manage to look as if you'd just stepped out of a crisp new wrapper after a day in this hell hole. A couple of hours in here used to make me feel as if I'd just been through a fight with an alligator in a particularly messy bit of swamp.'

`Nothing to it,' answered the girl, coolly. `I just pretend it's all part of a nasty dream and isn't happening to me at all.'

`That's one way,' replied Gunn. `Any idea what this is about.'

`Yes.'

`But you're not telling.'

`No, but I'm glad you're here. For a moment on the phone I thought you meant it.'

`I did,' said Gunn. `I've come to listen, nothing more.'

`Well, at least that's something. Being a retired sloth doesn't really suit you though - and you're putting on weight.'

`I am not,' said Gunn. `I weigh precisely what I have always weighed.' He pointed at a leather-covered door beyond her desk. `Is he in there?'

Polly nodded. `Yes, and you'd better go straight in. I've just about run out of excuses for you, and he's madder than a wet hen.'

`I'm not personally acquainted with many wet hens,' said Gunn. `So the sight should prove educational.'

The girl put a hand on his arm. `Seriously, Maxim. Something is worrying him badly. It might be a good idea to save the smart remarks.'

Gunn glanced at her in mild surprise and looked thoughtful. He'd never known her to advise caution where Vileman's blood pressure was concerned. He unhitched himself from the door jamb, walked to the door of the Chief's inner sanctum, thumbed the buzzer and without waiting for an answer, went in.

Casimir Vileman - the name was a version of an old Bohemian one, mistakenly Anglified by his great grandfather - was the director of a little known arm of the government's covert operations, simply known as the Organization. Other arms had names or letters and numbers like MI6 or Special Branch, but the Organization did not have official recognition: it didn't really exist, and Vileman was responsible to only one person - the Prime Minister of the day, and he did his job with an efficiency that earned him no friends, but great respect. As Gunn came in, he pointed wordlessly to a chair in front of his desk. Gunn sat down, crossed his legs and waited, surveying the man who had been his immediate superior with mild distaste, and with definite curiosity.

`Ever hear of Professor Edouard Shrinkker?' asked Vileman.

Gunn remained silent for a dozen heartbeats, thinking, and then answered. `Paris symposium on psychokinesis, telekinesis and the rest. Caught a lot of bad press and was practically laughed out of the city. Some crackpot theory about being able to control thought over a long distance. An extension of ESP and Psyonics, that kind of thing.'

Vileman raised his eyebrows in reluctant admiration.

`Quite right, Mr Gunn. Go to the top of the class. But that's not all. His claims went further than the usual ESP and stage mind-reading you hear about. Shrinkker really did mean control, with a capital `C'. He wasn't talking about just `influencing' or reading thoughts, and that's what got his peers so steamed up.'

`Sounds like a mixture of professional jealousy and sour grapes,' replied Gunn.

`More than likely. It seems that they couldn't face the possibility that someone really might have come up with the goods when all they'd been doing for years was footling about in the bushes.'

`And had he - come up with the goods?'

`Apparently so. Anyway, there was enough evidence for someone to get very interested. Interested enough to provide a lot of money for him to continue his work in seclusion.'

`And where was that?' asked Gunn.

`That's what I want to find out. I must know exactly where he is, who's behind him, and why.' Vileman swung his chair round and looked out onto the darkened street below. `All those millions of people out there; most of them wouldn't believe a tenth of what really goes on. Most of it's just story-book fiction to them, straight out of the last episode of the Twilight Zone.'

Gunn looked at his back curiously. He was seeing a new side to Vileman, a worried side, and he didn't much care for it.

`Care to tell me about it?' he said. `I presume that's why I'm here.'

Vileman swung back, rubbed tired eyes, and then became brisk as he pulled a bulging folder from a drawer.

`Right. The Prof went back to Salzburg, smarting at the insults and mumbling strange threats. And then he disappeared - literally. Just upped and left everything; his job at the university, his house - sold, the lot, and nothing more was seen or heard of him for nearly a year. A couple of months ago one of our men spotted him coming out of an hotel, in Ankara.'

`Who was that?' asked Gunn.

`Bill Henderson,' Vileman replied. `He contacted us in

the usual way and asked permission to follow up. He got it, of course, as we had Shrinkker marked for special attention if he showed up.'

Gunn did a quick mental flashback to Vileman's remark about the Twilight Zone. What the man said was true, things of that kind did get red flagged. The para-sciences had been knocking at some very strange doors in the last few years, some which he personally felt were better left unopened, but the facts remained. Just suppose that what this man Shrinkker was doing really worked, where would it lead? Spy satellites, sophisticated surveillance techniques and the whole mess of modern espionage would be wiped out in the blink of an eye. Double agents, treachery and blackmail would all be consigned to the stories of Le Carre and Deighton. There would be no need if you could just tune in to someone's thoughts, and then implant your own wishes. He came back with a jolt at the sound of Vileman's voice.

`We got a couple of progress reports. It seemed he was on to something, and I was expecting another.'

And then,' said Gunn, sensing the worst.

`And then I got these photos in the mail,' replied Vileman, and took a couple of Polaroid instant snapshots from the file. He passed them across the desk.

One photo showed a figure, dressed in nothing but a pair of shorts, lying spread-eagled at the base of a cliff. The surrounding ground was barren and stony, and the body lay in an unnatural broken doll attitude. It had obviously fallen off the cliff, or been pushed.

The second photo was a more distant shot, apparently for effect. It showed the cliff, a perpendicular drop of about three hundred feet. The body showed as a microscopic pale dot at the base. Gunn looked up at Vileman.

`Bill?'

Vileman nodded.

`Why was he dressed in just a pair of shorts in the

middle of the desert; and has an attempt been made to get a fix on the cliff?'

`There are a couple of leg men on that right now, making the rounds, questioning anyone who knows that part of the world; and we've called in the Geographical Society. They're looking at Turkey and down into Syria, Iran and Iraq. They may come up with something. But in the meantime this is as much as we know, and it'll make your hair curl.'

Gunn sat back and prepared to listen.

CHAPTER THREE

It took Vileman nearly two hours to give Gunn all the information so far collected, together with his own inferences and speculations, and to relay the Prime Minister's unequivocal instructions as to what was required from the Organization. Gunn could imagine the conversation that had taken place, briefly, over the red telephone on Vileman's desk, and was very glad he was no longer on the receiving end.

But the end result would be the same, this he knew. Vileman had called him in, come to him, almost cap in hand, because of those instructions. There had been one other in the Organization capable of doing what he knew was going to be asked of him, and Bill Henderson was lying dead, a broken doll at the foot of a three hundred foot cliff. Vileman was desperate, and he needed Gunn's help.

When Vileman finally finished and softly closed the file on his desk, Gunn had a clear vision as stark and as monstrous as anything he'd imagined in his wildest nightmares.

Only a little while before, a few months at most, he'd imagined that those ghosts were laid forever. Only the ghosts, it seemed, were not laid. They were creeping out again from the poisonous shadows where they had festered; made stronger and more savage by their earlier frustrations, and preparing for yet another attack on the bodies and minds of mankind.

The spectres of the past, of Hitler and Napoleon, were nothing in comparison to what this power might achieve, for they had only physical strength; they had never controlled the mind and spirit.

Gunn wondered with a suppressed shudder if they, or rather she, was truly human. He shook himself to rid his thoughts of such dark and unhealthy fantasies.

`Is that enough to be going on with?'

Gunn looked across the desk with narrowed eyes. `Enough? I believed she'd been killed at the Schloss. And now you tell me she is alive.'

`So we all thought,' replied Vileman. `But it seems she got away.'

`We dropped a damned great mountain on them. I saw it. Hundreds of thousands of tonnes of rock. A cock-roach couldn't have got out of that alive.'

Vileman shrugged, at a loss for an explanation.

`Which ones beside her?' asked Gunn. `Confirm my worst fears.'

`Wanda Liszt and the Baron for certain - Henderson saw them.'

Gunn silently digested the information for a moment, and then Vileman went on. `There's something going on that I just don't understand.'

`Such as,' Gunn asked.

`We know it's impossible that Wanda Liszt and the others got out of that collapse.'

`And yet they did you say. Bill saw them.'

`I know.'

`Why wasn't I told right away?'

`It wasn't your business,' Vileman replied. `You'd resigned, remember?'

`Anything about that woman is my business,' said Gunn, harshly.

`You'd be the first to agree with "need to know".'

`True,' Gunn admitted. `You said impossible in a peculiar way. What are you trying to say?'

`I'm not sure I'm trying to say anything,' said Vileman. `But I'm thinking, and I don't care for the thoughts.'

`Reasons?' Gunn asked.

`You'd laugh at me - or worse.'

`Try me. We haven't always agreed, but I've never ignored your ideas.'

Vileman gave him a thin smile and asked `When the impossible happens, what do you call it?'

`Blind luck,' said Gunn, firmly.

`Seriously.'

`O.K. A miracle.'

`Those things only happen for good people,' said Vileman. `What are they for people like her?'

`You tell me,' said Gunn. `I'm not in the mood for guessing games.'

`How about Black Magic - Witchcraft?'

Gunn's eyebrows shot up, and he bit back a laugh. `Be serious. Are you suggesting Wanda did this by ...?' He shook his head. `No. You can't be serious.'

Vileman's face told him that he was, and there was a strained quality in the set of his mouth that made Gunn cut off the smart remarks he might have made. Instead he said.

`Maybe you'd better tell me what this is all about. In my book, that kind of thing is the product of sick minds and wishful thinking - a lot of mumbo jumbo. But it seems it isn't in yours.'

Vileman looked acutely unhappy. `Listen Gunn. A month ago I'd have agreed with you, and I'd have recommended anyone who didn't to go and see a loony doctor. Now, I'm not so sure.' He paused for a while, marshalling his thoughts, and then went on. `You didn't go back to the Schloss after the collapse.'

`Your orders,' said Gunn. `Get away from the scene of the crime before the Swiss saw me, you said.'

Vileman nodded. `Yes. But the Chief of Staff did, and he noticed some funny things.'

`Such as?'

`A lot of ground had been moved - pushed aside, he

said; and it was right about where they would have been.'

`Somebody got there and lifted them?'

Vileman shrugged. `I don't know. But we did a lot of digging around, and there was no sign of Wanda or the other two. We found Kerstan, and that freak - Tinkerbell, but not the others.'

Gunn's face was grim. `Again, why wasn't I told?'

`Same answer. Need to know. You were on your way out by then, and had more important things on your mind.'

Gunn was forced to accept the logic. `O.K. But the fact that you didn't find them doesn't mean they weren't there. It was a hell of an explosion. They could have been thrown yards away.'

Vileman shook his head, and Gunn knew, deep inside, that it was so. Somehow Wanda had got away - or been removed, with the others.

`So what happened then,' he asked.

`I've no idea. Except this Shrinkker thing. It wasn't his theories about psychokinesis and ESP that got him laughed at, as I said. It was what he added to it; that he had found a way to control the supernatural forces. Up to that point he had been taken fairly seriously - but that did it. Exit Shrinkker in a cloud of laughter and abuse.'

Gunn felt his mouth twitching with humour despite himself, and asked. `You think they - someone - took the body, or bodies away, and somehow brought them back to life? It's a bit far-fetched.'

Vileman sighed. `Far-fetched, yes. But whether it's impossible, I don't know. People get themselves frozen these days; cryogenics or whatever, don't they? They hope some miracle of medicine will come up, and they'll be brought back to life. If that could happen, why not this? Hell, Gunn,' he said, exasperated. `I don't know, but I need to. The damned woman is out there, and so are the others, and according to Bill Henderson, they're hatching up this thing. They've got to be stopped. It's got to be stopped. And now they've turned up in Ankara - or Turkey at any rate.'

Gunn got up and walked to the door. `I'd better get started then'.

Vileman gave him an odd smile. `I didn't ask, yet.'

`But you were going to,' said Gunn.

`Yes.'

`Then I've just saved you the bother.'

`May I ask why? A few months ago you swore you'd never do anything like this ever again.'

`It's just this once,' replied Gunn quietly. `You might call it unfinished business. And besides,' he added. `Bill Henderson was my friend.'

`What are you going to do? I mean, you may be doing this as a favour, or for personal reasons - I don't much care which, but it's my head on the block in the end.'

Gunn smiled at the thought. `I'm not sure, but there are a couple of people I want to talk to, and Polly's got to get things organized from this end. I'll contact you in the usual way when I get to Ankara. By the way, can I have what I want, all the way?'

Vileman nodded. `Even to half my kingdom. Just pull it off.'

Gunn went out and closed the door softly behind him.

Polly Anders was still waiting as he came out, somehow still managing to look as bright and fresh as a new rose, despite the fact that she'd been there all day and it was then well past midnight.

`Are you going to do it?' she asked.

Gunn nodded. `It seems there are a couple of loose ends.'

The girl pulled a face. `Some loose ends. How did she get out Maxim?'

Gunn shrugged. `They say the Devil looks after his own.'

`Where do you start?'

`Turkey,' he replied. `But to get things in the right order. First, coffee; second, all available information on Professor Edouard Shrinkker, and then book me on a flight to Ankara. Oh, and a room - no, make that a suite - at the Buyuk Ankara Hotel. There's an afternoon flight with Turkish Airlines which will get me there in time for dinner. Have you an office I can use?'

Polly gave him a wry smile. `Your old one is still empty. And, of course, there's Bill's.'

Gunn stood in the doorway of his old room and switched on the light. It was just an empty room. Gone were the few personal possessions, now at his home, which had given the place a personality. The silver cigarette box - an unlikely gift from the K.G.B. A Malay kris inscribed with the ninety-nine names of God, and a paper weight made from a bronze arrowhead. All mementos of people and places in his past. And there was a lighter patch on the wall where a lithograph of Basil Rathbone as Sherlock Holmes used to hang, which some might have thought was vanity, but would not have dared to say so.

He sat down in the swivel chair, put his feet on the desk and closed his eyes, thinking.

The first shock of discovering that Wanda Liszt was alive had passed, to be replaced by an almost irrational excitement. God knows, he'd wished her permanently out of the way many times, and on two occasions had done his best to see that it had happened; but he had to admit that life without her had begun to be just the tiniest bit dull. He knew he would never return to use this room as a right; but just maybe he could start to borrow it once in a while. He had retired from the game, that much was certain, but there was nothing in his promise to say he couldn't consult.

There was a knock on the door and he dropped his feet to the carpet with a thud as the records clerk came in with a bulky file and a docket to sign. Gunn scribbled his signature, knowing he would not be allowed out of the building again until the file was returned, and checked. His watch showed it was nearly one o'clock. He thought he would just read the file to get the gist and reinforce what Vileman had told him, and then go home for some sleep. It was too late to do anything else, and Wanda Liszt could wait a few hours.

Polly Anders brought his coffee: hot, strong, black and sweet, as he liked it. He grinned at her, boyishly.

`How are the mighty fallen,' she said, with a satisfied smirk.

`And just what is that supposed to mean?'

`You swore you'd never come back.'

`I haven't.'

`But I see you, sitting in that chair.'

`A one-off job. Like I said, loose ends.'

`I believe you,' the girl said. `And I suppose that's why you dropped the fishing holiday so quickly, and you're sitting there with a Cheshire Cat grin. You couldn't stay away, could you?'

Gunn frowned at her. `Would you, with Wanda Liszt back from the dead?'

Polly poured him coffee and placed it carefully on the blotter in front of him. `How did she get out of that one, Maxim?'

Gunn rubbed his chin, thoughtfully. `I must remember to ask her when I see her. Now you'd better push off, Polly. You must be beat. And besides, you've got to be fresh for that lunch you owe me.'

`Just you see that you're around to collect,' she replied. `Or I'll never speak to you again.'

Gunn stayed in the office for another hour before calling records and returning the file to the clerk, during which time he had skimmed through the information available on the dubious professor - and there was quite a lot. The red tag had meant a continuous updating since the Paris symposium; but Gunn's phenomenal powers of concentration and acute memory had taken in more than anyone else would have found possible in the time.

The file contained notes and reports from many sources and in several languages, including Russian, German and French - all of which he read and spoke with total fluency, but nowhere was there any clue as to where the man had gone to ground. True, he had last been seen in Ankara, and that was where the trail would have to be picked up. But apart from that Gunn was going to be looking for a small needle in a vast haystack. And the devil of it was that he didn't know how much time he had. Vileman had given him the end product of Wanda's intentions, but without a location he was going to have to rely on a large slice of luck.

He left the office and walked slowly out of the building, having returned the file, and stopped briefly to say goodnight to the man who had replaced Magoon for the night shift. Ex-Marine Commando O'Rourke looked admiringly after the tall, elegant figure as he went out of the doors. He envied Magoon who had been on the Swiss job with him. Maybe one day he'd be sent along to lend a hand. God knows, he was a useful man in a scrap too, and he'd proved it a dozen times in some pretty sticky situations.

Gunn went out into the warm night, and stood for a few moments on the pavement before getting into his car. Tomorrow in Ankara it would be hot.

The Lagonda responded instantly to the starter, and he drove across the City and into the West End. Five minutes brought him to his house in Clarges Street, and he parked in his usual place.

As he mounted the steps to his front door, key in hand, it swung open to reveal the imperturbable Sweetstory, his man, and friend.

`Good evening, Sir,' said Sweetstory, without emotion.

`Good evening,' replied Gunn. `I thought you'd be in bed hours ago.'

`Miss Anders telephoned, Sir, and informed me of your return.'

`The blessings of Allah on her.'

`Indeed, Sir. Your bath is ready should you wish it.'

`Thank you, Sweetstory.'

`Thank you, Sir. The fish were biting satisfactorily I trust.'

`Adequately.'

`I am gratified, Sir. Will that be all, Sir?'

`Yes, thank you.'

`Good night, Sir.'

`Good night, Sweetstory,' said Gunn, and walked up the stairs to his bedroom.

CHAPTER FOUR

The morning was bright and clear when Gunn left his house the following day and there was promise of a real scorcher to come.

He strode into Piccadilly and turned towards the Circus. Normally he would have taken his car, but where he wanted to go parking could be a real problem, and anyway, he felt like the exercise. He glanced at his watch and noted with satisfaction that there was ample time to visit two potentially useful people before keeping his lunch date with the Lady Cynthia Ffoote.

Cynthia Ffoote was an enigma to Gunn's friends, and the nearest thing to a permanent girl friend his peculiar life allowed. Those who knew him had reckoned he would marry her after retiring from the Organization, but when the question was raised he merely smiled and shrugged. She was beautiful, she was charming, she was rich, and it was quite obvious that she adored the lean, hard adventurer; but equally, she made no demands on him, and that was undoubtedly important to him.

As he passed the Ritz Hotel he briefly noted the polyglot cast of guests getting out of and getting into taxis, and unlike most people who thought that London's individuality was being melted down, he thought it was becoming more interesting. There were people from so many lands and speaking so many languages, that it was sometimes possible to forget where you were for a few minutes; and he also got amusement from being able to understand a great deal of what was being said, no matter what language it was in.

He passed through Leicester Square and on into the Charing Cross Road, and minutes later turned up a dingy side alley and went into a book shop which displayed a dog-eared selection of rubbish in the dirty window, and a hopeful sign which stated that "Rare Books" were bought and sold.

An old-fashioned bell above the door tinkled as he pushed it open and went into the gloomy interior. There was a mingled smell of dusty decay, spicy food, and something that suggested incense. He walked past the glass-topped counter and through a beaded curtain. Then he coughed and called quietly.

`Rudy? It's Maxim. Stop counting your shekels for a moment and come and talk to me.'

There was a startled exclamation from the back of the darkened interior, and a gnarled figure in a kaftan and round black cap moved out of the gloom and thrust a bearded face at him.

`No need to count, young man. I know to the last one how many there are. And what can you want of an old man like me? I suppose you're in trouble again and want old Termaxian's help.'

`No trouble, Rudy,' laughed Gunn. `But I do want your help. I need information.'

Rudolph Termaxian was a man of uncertain age, more uncertain origin - though he liked to say he was an Armenian Jew - and of undoubtedly uncertain reputation. What was certain though, was that he knew more about the secret and unknown ways of the world than any man alive. Gunn had earned his friendship many years before during some unpleasant incidents in the old man's homeland, and had been the means by which his life - considered worthless, and his fortune - considered enormous, had been saved. Ever since that day he had looked on Gunn as a son, or favourite nephew at least, and had remained one of his most valuable sources of information.

Gunn sat down on a faded upright chair which had the unmistakable look of being Louis XIV, and probably was, and placed the glass of tea which had materialized on the Hepplewhite table at his side.

`Rudy,' he asked. `What do you know of Wanda Liszt?'

`Not as much as you I think, my Maxim. With the possible exception of one thing. She is still alive and did not die at the Schloss Swartzrabe.'

`I found that out yesterday,' replied Gunn, sourly.

`Together with the Baron, and de Lorian?'

`Yes, them also.' Gunn tilted the chair back on two legs and gazed at the dark ceiling. He let the chair drop forward and looked hard at the old man. `And what about a certain Professor Edouard Shrinkker, does his name ring any bells?'

`Again, probably not as much as with you, except that someone began to show a great interest in him about a year ago. And then he suddenly vanished.'

`And, of course, you would have no idea where he is,' added Gunn with a smile.

Termaxian made a maybe-maybe-not gesture with his hand. `Only vaguely.'

`Which means you can't remember the telephone number,' said Gunn, dryly.

`Which means I can only put it in a general area,' replied Termaxian, smoothly. `More detail you can probably obtain from an old friend of mine in Ankara.'

`So he's still in Turkey?'

`Surely you knew that. Anyway, I'll tell you about this friend before you leave. I do not know what Shrinkker is doing, however, though he made some unusual claims in Paris - which I am sure you know about, and given the megalomanic delusions of that Lady, the two could make a combination which is the stuff of which nightmares are made.'

`Shrinkker is with Wanda Liszt. You are sure?'

The old man sipped his tea and cocked his head to one side, looking at Gunn like a wicked sparrow. `I am sure. But I thought you were no longer part of that world, Maxim.'

`I'm not,' Gunn replied, firmly. `But it seems there is unfinished business if they are still alive.'

`And you work for this Vileman again?'

Gunn shook his head. `Not officially. This is by way of a favour.'

Termaxian chuckled. `So, the good life was getting boring.'

`It's a one-off job,' said Gunn. `After this, no more.'

`Of course. Do you know what they are up to this time?'

Gunn nodded. `I have a fair idea.'

`And it is to do with what Shrinkker was doing?'

`It is,' Gunn replied.

Termaxian leaned forward and put his hand on Gunn's knee. `Then put an end to it, Maxim. The secret probably still lies within the man's brain. I too have heard whispers, of a machine. Destroy the machine and another will be built. You must destroy the man and the machine. He is a poor deluded fool and no doubt believes he will be rewarded for his genius. Bah! His reward will be a bullet in the head; but not until they have what they want. And there is another rumour; that Wanda Liszt has sold herself into partnership, and it is not with the Americans.'

Gunn raised an eyebrow. `Really. Then maybe she has bitten off more than even she can chew this time.'

Gunn finished his tea, which had by then gone cold. `Do you have someone I can contact in Ankara?'

`Yes,' said Termaxian. `His name is Nikolai Rostov, the son of a Tsarist emigré. Rumour has it that he is a Grand Duke or some such thing, but I do not believe it. He maintains an appearance of impoverished splendour, made all the more pathetic by the holes in his shoes and the dirt under his nails. Be that as it may, I call him friend, and his sources of information and his ability to produce forbidden articles is nearly as good as mine.'

`How will I find him?' asked Gunn.

`No doubt you will be staying at the Buyuk Ankara Hotel. Yes? Then he will find you.'

Termaxian gave Gunn a worried look, and said. `I think perhaps there are other things you should know, my friend, before you leave here. I have heard rumours.'

Gunn said nothing, and waited for the old man to continue.

`You have had dealings with this woman before, my friend; and that should have told you that she long ago sold her soul to the Devil - and I do not say that lightly. There are things about her that are beyond normal understanding.'

Gunn was surprised at the old man's attitude, and the respect and the hint of fear that crept into his voice as he spoke, and he felt a chill prickle the hairs on the back of his neck as he recalled Vileman's words of the night before.

`What are you getting at?' he asked.

Termaxian was reluctant to elaborate at first, but Gunn pressed and he answered. `Have you ever thought how she, and the others, lived through the holocaust at the Schloss Swartzrabe?'

`No,' Gunn admitted. `I didn't know until last night that they had. Vileman asked me something similar and my answer was blind luck. The strength of those old walls must have created a cave of some sort. It's the only logical explanation.'

Termaxian shrugged. `Maybe. I hope logic is the answer. But somehow I think there is more to it than that.'

`Explain,' demanded Gunn, harshly. `There's something you're not telling.' He knew what was coming, or thought he did, and it bothered him, badly.

Termaxian rubbed his long nose, and the old, grey head waved to and fro like a wrinkled cobra's. `You would not believe it.'

`Try me.'

Again Termaxian demurred. `You are a man of the hard, practical world, Maxim. You deal in facts; situations that have logical, understandable explanations, however bizarre and distasteful they may be. This is something beyond that. This woman, and her allies, are beyond that, though their powers are limited.'

Gunn's eyes narrowed, and again he felt the hairs on his neck stir. Coincidence? Vileman and his old friend on the same track independently was too much for coincidence. He tried to dismiss the whole thing as absurd nonsense, but couldn't. Termaxian was afraid, and after what he'd been through in his long life, it took a lot to accomplish that. He leaned forward and touched the old man kindly on the knee.

`If I am to take her on, if I am to beat her at this game, I need to know. What is it about her that makes you like this?'

`Like what?' Termaxian asked, quickly.

`Afraid,' said Gunn.

Termaxian shuddered slightly, sighed and sat back.

`You are right. It is only fair. And you are like a son to me.' He got up and refilled their tea glasses before continuing.

`I said she had sold her soul to the Devil,' he repeated.

Gunn smiled. `The same could be said of a lot of others. Some have even said it of me.'

Termaxian made a small, irritated gesture. `I am serious, Maxim. I mean exactly what I said. The woman has exchanged her hopes of paradise for power - more power than you can dream of.'

`You really mean ...' Gunn began.

`Yes,' Termaxian snapped. `She is in league with the Devil.'

`There's no such thing, old friend. The Devil and Hell are the ravings of sick and deluded minds.'

Termaxian peered at him from beneath grey, shaggy brows, and Gunn saw the hint of a smile. `I am sick and deluded?'

`No. Dammit. You know what I mean.'

Termaxian nodded. `That there is no Devil?' He shrugged. `That is so. I use the name figuratively. But there is evil; a vast, untapped source of energy that only needs the right key, the right formula to release it.' He looked at Gunn questioningly. `You believe in the power of good?'

Gunn nodded. `Of course.'

`And how do you define it? What name do you give the power of good? Do you call it God?'

Gunn felt intensely uncomfortable. These kinds of questions and arguments were the ones he normally avoided. No facts, only beliefs and feelings. You could not argue the unprovable. `I suppose so,' he replied.

`Then by the physical laws of the Universe, for every action there is an equal and opposite reaction. For every plus there is a minus. The Universe and the powers in it must balance, or the result would be chaos. If you believe in a power of good, why do you not also believe in a power for evil?'

Gunn sighed. The question had no answer. The logic was inescapable, and yet he found it hard to accept. `You mean she has found a way to control that power?' he asked.

Termaxian shrugged. `Control may be too strong a word, for perhaps such things are uncontrollable. But with what she has got from Shrinkker, I think she can use it to a degree. You could say she has come to an arrangement in exchange for what is called her soul.'

Gunn exploded. `You mean the bloody woman's a witch?'

Termaxian's wrinkled face registered distaste. `A silly, medieval word, but in essence, yes. She has found powers that are beyond ordinary people, and that is what makes her so dangerous now.'

`But that's preposterous,' Gunn replied. But he said it without conviction.

`Listen, my friend,' said the old man. `Last year, at the Schloss, and before that, she was dangerous; but that danger was the result of her fine brain, brilliant planning, and the control she had over her people through sheer personality.'

`A lot of good it did her,' said Gunn, quietly.

Termaxian smiled. `That was your doing, Maxim. You were her nemesis. But in the last year she has changed - I hear things, you know. She has become more dangerous. Believe me, I do not say these things lightly.' He smiled sadly at Gunn. `There are more things in heaven and earth, Horatio, than are dreamt of in your philosophy. Hamlet was right I think.'

`You really are serious about this, aren't you,' said Gunn. `You really think Wanda Liszt has - powers - or whatever you want to call them.'

` I am deadly serious, Maxim. Go against her, and you are going against a greater danger than you can imagine.'

`So what do I do to guard myself against her? Last time we met she didn't seem more than ordinarily rotten. Holy water and crucifixes seem a bit melodramatic. By the laws of any land the woman is a criminal, but try bringing her to trial on a charge of witchcraft and see how far you get.'

Termaxian shook his head. `Do not scoff at the symbols of the Christian church - or any other righteous belief - my friend. Symbolic these things may be, but they are focal points for good, and that is what counts. Arm yourself with them and treat them seriously. Centuries of good faith have made them powerful.'

`You mean if I just waltz up and stick a crucifix in her face, she'll surrender?' Gunn asked, with a touch of amusement.

`That she will not. But they will help concentrate your mind, and that will help. In the meantime, use Rostov, there are certain things he may be able to do. Until then, keep a watch over your shoulder, and carry a revolver.'

`Should it have silver bullets?' Gunn asked, with a smile.

Termaxian again showed his irritation. `You must take what I say seriously. Go into this thing with the realization that the danger I speak of is very real. Treat it lightly, as the imaginings of a stupid old man, and you will fail - or worse. To fail with that woman will mean your death.'

Gunn's attitude changed and he became serious. `My friend. I have never ignored anything you have said, and will not this time. If you say there is danger, I believe you, no matter how fantastic it seems.'

Termaxian stood up and searched Gunn's face, looking for signs of truth; and then, apparently satisfied, he went to a mahogany desk at the back of the room, unlocked a drawer and took out a small wooden box, inlaid with mother of pearl, which he opened with a small key. Gunn watched curiously as he took out a primitively worked silver pendant on a chain. Termaxian gave it to him. `Wear this, at all times,' he said. `It will give you some protection.'

Gunn took it from his hand and held it to the light. It was round, about an inch and a half in diameter, and worked with symbols that were familiar to him; among them the eye of Horus, and a swastika. `A swastika?' he asked. `Surely that belongs to the other side.'

`Long before the Nazis usurped it, it was a very ancient Indian good luck symbol for the sun, and good luck. It has powers.'

`And the rest. What is it?'

`It was given to me by a holy man - many years ago - in the mountains beyond the Amu Darya, which used to be called the Oxus River. He told me it had been blessed by the eighth Dalai Lama, and would protect whoever wore it from evil. I wore it before coming to this country, and as you know I escaped. Take it, my friend. Part of the protection of all such things is belief - but who knows.'

Gunn was strangely touched as he hung the amulet around his neck, and the moment he tucked it inside his shirt, he felt an unaccountable relaxation of the tensions which had been building. Termaxian then wrote a name on a slip of paper, and said. `This man will contact you when you arrive in Ankara. This Rostov is a man of many parts, and uncertain origin, though there are those rumours.' Termaxian shrugged and smiled. `Personally, I think he is just a rogue; but he is useful and knows many things. Do not, however, trust him too much.'

Silently Gunn took the old man by the shoulders and smiled his thanks, and without another word walked quickly out of the room, through the shabby storefront and out onto the street.

As he stood on the sunlit pavement, he felt that somehow the brightness had gone out of the day, and shivered involuntarily. Evil is somehow understood, even expected in the dark hours of the night; but in the warm glow of a summer's day in the middle of one of the greatest cities of the world, with normal sounds and sights of people going about their business, it took on a more terrible aspect by being out of place and at odds with the surroundings. He touched his shirt front where the amulet lay concealed against his chest, and then in irritation put it out of his mind. Touch wood, don't walk under ladders - all rubbish. There had to be a logical explanation that would put Termaxian's warnings into perspective - but was there?

He shrugged, and turned in the direction of Trafalgar Square, and a short while later found himself at the doors of one of the Foreign Office departments - though it might have denied the association.

He walked through the door, climbed a flight of stairs between walls of uniformly dismal Ministry of Works brown, and knocking at a stippled glass door, went in. A middle-aged spinster type was seated at a wooden desk, somehow managing to knit an intricate Fairisle pattern and study a thick file at the same time. Gunn turned on his most charming smile and asked.

`Mr Quantrill in, Ma'am?'

The woman wilted visibly when she saw him. Her heart fluttered as she thought that this was what Sir Hereward Strongbow must have looked like - the hero in her latest Harlequin romance.

`Have you an appointment?' she squeaked. `Mr Quantrill doesn't see ..'

`Anyone without one,' Gunn finished. `I'm sure he'll make an exception in my case. The name's Gunn. Maxim Gunn.'

Miss Harlequin Fairisle got up and patted her hair into place. `Wait a moment,' she said. `I'll see if he's free.' She knocked on a door and went into the office beyond. Gunn could hear muted conversation, and then a bull-like voice roared.

`Of course I'll see him, Molly. If there's one man on earth I'll always see, it's Maxim Gunn. Wheel him in. On the double now. Quick march. One, two, one, two.'

Gunn smiled again at the flustered Molly as she came back pedalling out, and said, `Marvellous of you to arrange that at such short notice. Many thanks.' He stepped past her and went into the office.

Toby Quantrill shambled across the threadbare carpet like a huge, delighted bear and took Gunn's outstretched hand in a grip that made him wince.

`Come in, come in,' he roared. `Park yourself, me old china. Must be a couple of years since you've darkened these doors. What can I do for you? It is do, I suppose. You haven't just dropped in for a chat?'

Gunn sank gratefully into the one comfortable chair in the room. He felt like he always did when confronted by Quantrill: rather like a stook of corn that's just been through a threshing machine.

`No, Toby,' he smiled. `This is official; or as official as I can ever be. Which means I haven't been here and haven't said a word to you.'

`Gotcha.'

`Turkey. Or possibly Syria, and maybe even excursions over the borders into Iran and Iraq.'

`Largish sort of area, old man.'

`I realize that. In the past twelve months, have there been any covert movements of classified material or equipment? Dead of night kind of stuff. Turn your eyes to the wall my children. Most likely coming from the south, in boxes still stencilled with little crescents and stars, or maybe hammers and sickles for all I know. Not your usual rockets and general military gear, but really hush-hush.'

`What might these boxes contain. Or can't you tell me?'

`Computers. High frequency transmitting equipment. Electronic gadgetry of unspecified kinds. That kind of thing.'

Quantrill leaned back and pulled out a battered and stinking pipe.

`Off hand I can't call anything to mind - no, wait a minute. Little bell tinkling in the grey matter. Some funny stuff at the border just north of Zakho about that time. The guards were all set to make a stink about stuff coming through without papers, and then some ultra V.I.P. appeared and told them it wasn't there, and they hadn't even seen it. Nobody thought anything about it at the time. It didn't seem very important. One of our chaps who mooches around the area pretending to be a goatherd -

actually he is a goatherd, come to think of it - just passed it on as a matter of routine, and because it wasn't military stuff. Now there's a turn up for you. Nobody usually bothers to hide anything that doesn't go bang.' He buzzed his intercom. `Molly. Be a good girl and rustle out that report from Mustapha Kemel. Fishy things coming over the border. You remember? Came in about mid-July last year.'

The file with the report came in a couple of minutes, and Quantrill, perching a pair of half glasses on his nose, quickly thumbed through it, and then extracted a flimsy.

`Here we are,' he said. `Now let me see. Tenth July; late evening. A convoy of trucks carrying bulky, but not heavy crates passed through the border. Trouble started by the guards, but quickly stopped on arrival of high ranking brass, who had no doubt been suitably bribed. Eight trucks in all, and our man heard the name Bolkar Dag mentioned.' Quantrill glanced at Gunn. `That's a mountain range in the south near Adana. There's nothing down there but a lot of wild country. No military installations worth mentioning and precious little industry apart from tourism. Our fellow got a peek under one of the covers while chasing a stray goat - useful beggars, goats - and reckoned he saw something like a large generator and transformer before he got chased off.'

Gunn felt a quick surge of satisfaction. `That's marvellous, Toby,' he said. `Just the kind of information I was hoping for.'

`Blessed if I know why, old son. Doesn't sound much to go on, but I expect you know best. Not that you'd tell me anyway.' He smiled wistfully. `You know, one of these days I'd like to crack a bottle with you and get the low down on what you really do.'

`Nothing very exciting I'm afraid,' Gunn replied. `I'm just a sort of policeman really.' And with that he got up. `We must meet again a bit sooner next time. And this time didn't happen, remember? Thanks again. You've been a great help.'

`Mum's the word, old man.' And Quantrill smiled. `Maxim Gunn. Who's he?'

Gunn went through the outer office, threw another smile at Molly, saying. `He's a very lucky man, having you here, Ma'am.' And slipped out, leaving her glowing pinkly with pleasure.

He stopped on the pavement outside and checked his watch. Perfect; a brisk walk to give him an appetite, and he'd be dead on time for his lunch appointment with Cynthia at the Savoy Grill.

CHAPTER FIVE

The Turkish Airways jet banked as it began its approach into Ankara's Edenboga airport. Gunn heard the muted roar of the engines decrease as the throttles were eased back, and then the tell-tale whine of hydraulics as the flaps lowered. He opened his eyes, stretched and looked out of the window. It was evening, and the land below was a mass of dark, purpling shadows, twinkling with the lights of villages. He was totally relaxed and had none of the butterflies in the stomach so common to many air travellers. A brilliant pilot himself, qualified on most types of aircraft, civilian and military, he had supreme faith in the crew at the controls, knowing full well the rigid qualifications they possessed, and the endless hours of training and flight experience. Moments later the engines throttled back, and with a slight bump and shriek of tortured rubber, the plane landed and the jets went into reverse thrust.

Gunn was in no particular hurry, so he remained seated and let the eager ones file nose to tail down the gangway. They'd only have to wait in the customs hall, and he preferred the air conditioned comfort of the cabin.

Twenty minutes later, immigration and customs behind him, he carried his battered leather case out to the taxi rank, hailed the least decrepit looking vehicle, and gave the driver the name of the Buyuk Ankara Hotel. He was looking forward to a shower and dinner.

It was nearly nine o'clock when he took his coffee out onto the terrace of the hotel, feeling the world was really quite a pleasant place, especially, he had to admit, now that he was back doing a worthwhile job and not trying to behave as if there were no problems but his own.

Like most eastern cities, even though Turkey is part of Europe, Ankara does not go to bed early, and he thought that after the coffee he would take a stroll through the surrounding streets and savour the nostalgia of the sounds and smells.

He was seated at a small, round table, partially concealed by a cascading bougainvillaea, quietly enjoying the warm, scented evening, when he heard the low voices, and saw the silhouettes of a man and a woman coming through the gardens toward the terrace. The man bent attentively to the woman, who laughed lightly at some remark, and then they mounted the steps to the terrace and came into the light thrown from the hotel windows. The man was elegantly dressed in evening clothes, his white shirt gleaming. He was unknown to Gunn, who merely noted his presence and turned his attention to the woman. And then his face hardened into a mask, his pulse quickened, and he drew himself further back into concealment. The soft light showed a face of remarkable beauty, dark hair falling in soft waves to her shoulders in perfect contrast with the flawless white skin and equally white silk dress. Gunn swore softly to himself as he took in, once again, the dark beauty of Wanda Liszt.

The man took her elbow and said something, obviously inviting her into the hotel. Wanda Liszt shrugged lazily, inclined her head in acknowledgment, and they began to move across the terrace towards the door.

They drew parallel with Gunn, the man smiling encouragement to his lovely companion, when she suddenly stopped, brushed his hand off her arm, and slowly turned to Gunn's half hidden table. Gunn froze.

Ignoring her puzzled escort, she took a tentative step towards Gunn, peered intently for a moment at his shadowy form, and then, taking a deep breath, she bowed very slightly in his direction.

For the space of a dozen heartbeats their eyes locked,

and an unspoken message flashed between. This was not the place, or the time, but recognition was absolute. Then she turned quickly, took the man's arm and they disappeared into the bright room beyond the door.

Gunn let his breath out in a long sigh, and realized he had been holding it from the moment she had felt his presence. Then he sat back and picked up his cup with a steady hand, and a smile moved across his face briefly.

So, he thought, the cat was out of the bag. Mischance, or perhaps fate, had taken away any hope of surprise. He rejected immediately any hope that Wanda might put his presence down to coincidence. She knew why he was in Ankara as surely as if he had advertised it in banner headlines. One small thing wriggled insistently at the back of his mind however, clamouring for attention; how had she known he was there? Many people have a sixth sense for the presence of an unseen figure, that was explainable; but he knew she could not have seen his face in the shadow - and yet she had known it was him. A flicker of cold chased down his back, and despite himself he touched the amulet under his shirt.

Gunn reviewed the situation, suddenly changed by Wanda's inopportune appearance - or maybe, on second thoughts, it was opportune. She now knew where he was, and his instincts shouted that she would not sit idly back. Maybe he was saved the long search for clues that he would originally have undertaken, with no guarantee of success, as apart from the uncertain information that she was in Turkey, he had had nothing to go on. Now, at least he knew she was there. He decided to spend a couple of days playing the tethered goat and let the tiger attack him, keeping a very sharp eye on his back at all times.

He was about to get up and go for the stroll he had planned, when a waiter came up with a folded note on a tray, and the explanation that a messenger had left it at the desk. Gunn thanked him and unfolded the paper. It was from Rostov. Gunn raised an eyebrow and reflected that the Russian had certainly wasted no time, and the fact that the note was written in Russian indicated that the man certainly knew many things, as Termaxian had said. He wondered just how much of his past life was not quite as secret as he would have liked. The note suggested a meeting place and time for the following day. Gunn burned the page and scattered the ashes over the balcony, then swallowed his coffee and walked down the steps to the gardens towards a gate flanked by dusty palms and a thicket of oleander.

The attack was almost an anticlimax. Gunn spun and parried the blow effortlessly. The descending knife arm jarred against his raised forearm, causing the man to grunt with surprise. Gunn grabbed the wrist, turned and twisted. There was a loud snap and a single cry of pain, and the curved knife dropped to the gravel. He brought his right hand down in a vicious chop across the side of the exposed neck and felt the body go limp. He dropped the man, whirled and side-stepped as the weighted stick, carried by a second attacker, who had rushed out of the shadows, whistled harmlessly past his shoulder. Gunn leapt like a ballet dancer, and slammed the sole of his shoe against the man's jaw. It was no contest, and over almost before it had begun. He bent down and briefly examined the two unconscious forms, retrieved the knife and club. Hardly Wanda's style he thought; maybe just a couple of muggers after his wallet. But instinct told him not and he examined the knife more carefully. There was a dark, sticky substance on the blade. He touched it with the tip of his tongue and then spat quickly. It was curare, the paralyzing poison extracted from the South American woorali root. The knife man hadn't needed to stab him fatally, a mere scratch would have been enough. The attack in itself was nothing, a hazard that he had almost come to expect when he was operational with the

Organization; but Wanda Liszt had left the terrace not more than a quarter of an hour before, and the speed with which she must have organized it: attackers and poison, was something that made him respectful of her resources. Well, he'd been right, she hadn't wasted any time, though he seemed to have misread her message about time and place.

He straightened his tie thoughtfully and shrugged. Maybe he'd better forget about the stroll after all. God alone knew, but at this rate there might be characters lurking round every corner. Carefully, he stabbed the knife blade into the ground a dozen times to wipe off the poison, and then threw it into the nearest oleander clump before retracing his steps to the terrace and going up to his suite.

Taking off his clothes, he had a quick cold shower before putting on a towelling robe and opening his bottle of duty free Glenmorangie malt whisky; then he settled down to read a book he had picked up at Heathrow airport.

Some time later he was rudely shaken out of his peace by the most unholy racket coming from what seemed to be the suite next door. It sounded like a mixture between someone killing a pig and a minor riot, with a bit of furniture smashing thrown in for good measure. Gunn put down his book, crossed the room and cautiously opened the door onto the corridor.

There was a bellow of rage followed by a splintering noise as the door of the next suite crashed open. Gunn's eyebrows raised in mild surprise as a blonde giant emerged carrying at arms length, feet missing the ground by a good leg length, a small and obviously terrified man; his terror made all the more evident by the appalling noise he was making.

The giant dropped his squirming burden on the carpeted floor, drew back a ponderous foot, booted him a good ten yards and then turned and saw Gunn.

`A thief,' he explained mildly. `It's like this everywhere you go nowadays. If it's not nailed down you might as well kiss it good-bye.' He held out his hand and introduced himself. `Tornquist. Torquil Tornquist is the name.'

There was a patter of feet along the corridor and a posse arrived, consisting of the Manager, Under Manager, House Detective and assorted floor personnel, all talking at once, gesticulating, recriminating, apologizing and in general getting in each other's way. Tornquist brushed them aside like flies.

`The door appears to have come off its hinges as I was opening it,' he said, wonderingly. `Such shoddy workmanship these days. I will go down to the bar for one hour and then return.' He loomed over the manager. `It will be repaired by then, no?'

Gunn found himself strangely drawn to the man, and said. `You'd better come to my room instead. I've a bottle of malt whisky I'd like your opinion on.'

`So,' replied Tornquist, with a wide smile. `You think maybe the bottom half is not as good as the top half, eh? Very well, we shall find out.' He turned to the manager. `So, one hour, my friend. No more, eh?'

Tornquist went back into his suite to get a robe, and returned a minute later clad in scarlet silk, with a puzzled expression on his face and a large brown envelope in his hand. It was tightly sealed and bound with scotch tape.

`The thief, I think he dropped something,' he observed. `Let us look and see what it is.'

Back in his suite, Gunn poured them both drinks. Tornquist sipped his appreciatively, and said with a smile

`I think maybe we shall have to test the quality of this, what is it called, Glenmorangie? - just to make sure it is the same all the way to the bottom. And now for the envelope.' He slit it open, and taking out the contents, put them on the coffee table in front of him. After examining them in silence for a few minutes, he sat back and looked at Gunn quizzically.

`I think, my friend, that you are not all you seem to be.' He waved his hand at the scattered papers. `These would appear to be for you. I think perhaps I have done the little pig an injustice. He was not trying to steal from my room, but to put something in it.'

`And got the wrong room,' replied Gunn, without bothering to deny Tornquist's observation. Just occasionally he found it more helpful to tell the truth about himself, and he had a feeling that this was one of those times.

He picked up the papers and quickly sorted through them.

`I think you're right about the little visitor. Give me a few minutes to see what these are about, and then I'll tell you a story that'll curl your beard. I think another quality control sample from that bottle is in order, don't you?'

Twenty minutes later Gunn put the papers down, leant back and casually hooked a leg over the arm of his chair.

`I presume the quick look you had at that lot meant something to you,' he said.

`Something,' Tornquist admitted, `But not much. Though the name Edouard Shrinkker made me interested. I read something about him somewhere.'

`Your name means something to me also,' said Gunn. `Which is primarily why I'm going to tell you what I am. I think you may be able to help.'

`So,' smiled the Giant. `Tornquist is not altogether unknown. But you, my friend; what about you?'

`Let's just say I work for my government, and leave it at that. Explanations can be messy.' Gunn got up and went to the window, checked the curtains, and then sat down again. `This is what I think we're up against.'

By the time he finished, Tornquist was pacing the room like a caged lion, and had made a sizable dent in the Glenmorangie, with no visible effects on himself.

`Madame Curie said, "Nothing is to be feared, it is only to be understood," ' he quoted.

`Oh, sure,' Gunn replied. `But she wasn't talking about this kind of thing. Frankly, I don't understand this black magic stuff, and it scares me. Give me something I can see or get hold of, something I can punch on the nose or flatten with a bullet, and no matter how rough it gets I can usually cope; but this stuff gives me the willies.'

Tornquist shrugged massively. `Don't think of it like that, my friend. Think of it as a force which can be controlled if you know the right formulae and methods - like Curie's uranium. Frightening stuff if you are an ignorant layman, but nothing to worry about if you are a nuclear physicist.'

`Well, I'm a layman,' Gunn replied.

`So am I; but your friend, Henderson,' and Tornquist tapped the brown envelope. `His words in these papers show that it is a force, and one that this woman has brought under control. Not with spells or mixtures of dragon's blood and bat wings, but with computers, by God. The force obeys natural laws, as everything in the Universe must. Get to that computer of hers, smash it, destroy this Shrinkker, and her power is finished. Her powers must be limited too, or else why would she send thugs to kill you in the garden? If she had the great powers you are thinking of, would she not have sent some entity?'

`Maybe,' said Gunn, and there was a trace of doubt in his voice. `But first we've got to get at it, and that's going to be the difficult part if she's watching us all the way in her crystal ball.'

`I did not think you would be one to give up so easily,' said Tornquist, surprised.

Gunn mirrored his surprise. `I said nothing about giving up. I said it was going to be difficult.'

`Most things worth doing are; that's one of the reasons I am an archaeologist. It is a great challenge. A few clues, a small piece here and there, a tantalizing glimpse, and occasionally, just very occasionally a great truth emerges; and then it is all worthwhile.' Tornquist laughed delightedly and poured another majestic shot of whisky. `You, my friend, must feel as I do. Why otherwise would you have chosen the work you do? You could have signed on with some boring company and worked from nine to five - but you didn't.'

`Most of the time my work is boring and frustrating,' Gunn replied. `Probably like yours. But there are compensations.' He did not enlighten Tornquist to the fact that he was no longer a full-time operative, nor did he tell him the truth. His life with the Organization had never been boring, simply because he had never allowed himself to be dragged into the routine side of things. Paper work he had always left to others.

Tornquist refused to be deflated. `At least now we have a lead,' he said, excitedly. `It sounds like some wild tale from the Sagas; evil stalking the world.' He swung round and jabbed a finger at Gunn. `How well do you know the area of the Bolkar Dag Range?'

`Not at all,' Gunn replied. `I've never been there.'

`So. I have been up and down that area for the past few years; digging and searching, for as you know I am a great archaeologist.' Gunn smiled at the man's presumption. `I think I can say I know the area as well as any man who was not born there. Tell me, have you heard of Gilgamesh?'

`The Legend of Gilgamesh?' asked Gunn. `The mythical king? But surely he was Babylonian. This is Turkey.'

`Correct. But he was no myth, he did indeed live, and my theory is that he came north from his capital at Uruk at the end of his time, probably travelling along the Euphrates. There are certain pointers if you dig deep enough. Maybe he is now classified as legend, but that is only because we have few facts. But even the most improbable legends are based on fact. Look at Atlantis, Lemuria, King Solomon's Mines and Eldorado. I have theories about them, too. Sometimes the origin is lost forever, but there was one.'

Gunn was puzzled by the turn in the conversation. `What has all this to do with what I'm looking for?'

`Just this,' replied Tornquist. `For these people to have gone to earth so thoroughly, they must have gone underground. There are no man-made structures in that area of the size they would need, or that would provide the secrecy. Maybe they have found a cavern, or a tomb. Who knows, maybe the tomb of Gilgamesh.'

Gunn laughed. `All very fascinating, I'm sure, and maybe you're right; but looking for lost tombs, and trying to find out about Wanda Liszt, are two different things. I don't know how much time I've got, but certainly not enough for archaeology.'

Tornquist showed signs of impatience. `You miss the point, my friend. Find the one and I think you find the other.'

Gunn shrugged. `So, we go down to the middle of the mountains to look - we don't know where - for a cavern that may or may not be there. Should be simple. Any genius, with the luck of the devil could pull it off, no trouble.'

`You have a better suggestion perhaps?' Tornquist replied, frostily.

`I have no suggestion. Right now all I have is a picture of a cliff, and the fact that some highly suggestive equipment went to that area about a year ago.'

Tornquist looked smug. `So, let us go and look for it. A cliff should not be too difficult to recognize. And I, my friend, may kill two birds with one stone. I have been meaning for years to test my theory about Gilgamesh -

perhaps this is my opportunity, perhaps the gods are now pointing me in this direction no?'

When Torquil Tornquist returned to his suite, trailed by an apologetic manager, Gunn remained seated in a thoughtful frame of mind.

The mysterious package had been Bill Henderson's legacy, and contained some leads he hadn't bothered explaining to the Swede, and they made Gunn think that, just perhaps, Wanda's hideout and this Gilgamesh thing did have a connection, which in itself was intriguing but not relevant. He was reluctant to get Tornquist more involved, but he needed his knowledge, and in any case he had the look of a man who could take care of himself. If he was right, legend or not, then the area had to be combed, and his expertise would be invaluable.

In the meantime there was equipment to organize, and the appointment with Rostov. Termaxian had said the man was a rogue, but also a mine of information, apart from being able to lay his hands on certain needed items. For instance, there had been no possibility of bringing firearms with him, and he was going to need them.

It was with those thoughts that Gunn went to bed, and slept.

CHAPTER SIX

High above the desolation that was the Bolkar Dag, the fast moving lights of an aircraft winked against diamond bright stars. It was seen and heard by no-one except a lonely shepherd tending a flock of goats, and he was not interested. It passed over a range, disappearing from his view, but if he could, he would have identified the thudding beat of its engine as a helicopter.

Some minutes later, when its passing was no more than a memory for the shepherd, it loomed suddenly like a giant insect over the top of a great cliff, silhouetted briefly against the star studded sky, and then descended cautiously, its landing lights stabbing downward, towards a rough cut pad at the base of the cliff.

As the turbine whine of the engine died to a muted groan, the passenger door opened and a figure, dressed in a long coat against the night chill, got out and moved swiftly towards the cliff face. There was a rumbling sound, a square of light appeared, and the figure went inside. Then the rumble was repeated, the light narrowed and vanished, and darkness returned.

Wanda Liszt stood for a moment at the end of a long rock walled tunnel. She unbuttoned her coat and removed her gloves, speaking sharply to two men who were standing at rigid attention, their faces masks. Then she lifted her chin determinedly and swept along the tunnel, her booted feet echoing angrily. At the end of the tunnel she swung right at a junction, pushed violently through large double doors which slammed shut behind her, and entered a room that was in total contrast to the starkness of the rough hewn tunnel.

In what had once been a royal burial chamber, and was now an elegantly decorated drawing room, the Baron von Gilderstein sat at ease in a modern white leather armchair. The Baron was drawing with appreciation on a fine Havana cigar, while in his other hand he held a crystal balloon glass of cognac. He leapt to his feet as Wanda entered, spilling brandy on his trousers, and ineffectually trying to dab at it with the hand that held the cigar. The result was confusion.

`My God,' he said. `You gave me a fright. I thought you were in Ankara.'

She said nothing, but her face, a tight mask of fury, spoke volumes. The Baron continued, uncertainly.

`Something is wrong. You look like you've seen a ghost.'

Slowly Wanda Liszt regained her composure, colour came back to her cheeks and her breathing slowed. She pointed to a table where drinks were laid out, and the Baron hurried to pour her a glass of champagne. She took it from him wordlessly, drained it at a gulp, shrugged off her coat and threw it on a chair, then lit a cigarette.

`Maxim Gunn,' She spat the name as if it was a curse.

The Baron's jaw dropped, and he paled. `What? Here?'

She shook her head and held out the glass for a refill.

`No. In Ankara.'

`You saw him?'

She nodded. `And he saw me.'

`Then he knows you are alive.'

She gave him a contemptuous look.

`What happened?' the Baron asked.

`Then? Nothing. Later I tried to have him killed.'

`Tried?'

`Oh, for God's sake, Baron, spare me. I tried and failed.'

The Baron let out a long, slow sigh, drained his own

glass and refilled it. He was a worried man. Part of that worry was the news of Maxim Gunn, enough to worry anyone with the reputation he had; but his real worry was the Lady who stood before him. At one time he had been very respectful of her, afraid of her anger, even as he had been of her father before her. But since her rescue from burial and death at the Schloss, and the mind-numbing events that had led to her being brought back to life, she had taken on an aspect that took him beyond respect and into the realms of fear. She was playing with forces outside his understanding; forces he had previously shied from as impossible, even mythological, and she had gained control of them through the Professor's computers.

After the terrifying collapse of the Schloss; after the last rumble of thundering masonry had ceased and the fire and dust had settled, he had discovered to his amazement that he was still alive, and so was the woman de Lorian. Somehow the ancient stonework had formed a small arched cave; cramped to be sure, and dark as the pit of hell, but they were alive and there was breathable air.

How long they had lain entombed he never knew: hours or maybe days, his mind had drawn a veil across events it did not wish to remember. Dimly he recalled lights and voices and the sound of stone being dragged aside, and then he had been pulled into the open and had felt the blessed cool of fresh air on his face - then his mind had gone black. Later de Lorian, incredibly tough, mentally and physically for her age, had told him what had happened.

They had been rescued, by a couple of the original crew who had survived the explosion outside the walls, and then she, de Lorian, had organized a safe hiding place and had seen to it that Wanda Liszt's body was cryogenically frozen until she could contact the one person who might help. Professor Edouard Shrinkker might have been reviled as a crank by his peers, but not by her, and not by Wanda, who had felt all along that they might use his discoveries one day. That day had come, but not at that time in the way envisioned.

Shrinkker had been found, had been persuaded and coerced, and had finally agreed to try. The first two attempts to bring Wanda Liszt back to life had been failures; there had been errors in his calculations that had given them all some terrifying moments. But he had got it right in the end; the forces had been harnessed, albeit reluctantly, and the Baron had been in the great chamber when he had seen the miracle happen. Wanda's lifeless corpse had twitched like a puppet with the strings being tugged, then she had started to breathe, and finally, as he watched in open-mouthed shock, her eyes had suddenly opened and he had seen consciousness and awareness flood back into their dark depths. The impossible had happened. Wanda Liszt had been raised from the dead.

But something else had also happened. Something had taken part of her soul, and looking into her eyes sometimes gave him the nightmarish sensation that another presence was sharing her body; that she was not alone in there. She must have been aware that this had happened, because in an instant her eyes would change as if shutters were slammed - and she would smile secretly.

`What are we going to do?' he asked. He felt out of his depth and wanted guidance.

Wanda Liszt was puzzled. `Do? We carry on, Baron.'

`And Gunn?' he asked.

Her face hardened, and he got a momentary glimpse of the other presence. `We kill him,' she hissed.

However much he agreed with her, the Baron was shaken by the hatred in her voice, and he tried to reassure her, and himself.

`Nothing links us to this place, my Lady. He cannot possibly find us.'

Wanda made a sound of pure animal fury, and he winced as she rounded on him. `Spare me such childish ravings, Baron. He will find us. I feel it, here.' And she slapped her hand against her breast. `Somehow we have slipped up - but how?' And then understanding dawned and her eyes widened. `God, I'm a fool.'

`My dear?' said the Baron, puzzled.

`My foolish pride. The photographs, of the man Henderson. I sent them to Vileman. Somehow he must have identified the place.'

`Impossible,' said the Baron, firmly. `A cliff is a cliff. It could be anywhere in the world. But it doesn't explain Gunn's presence. He has nothing to do with Vileman any longer.'

Wanda sat down quickly. `I wonder,' she breathed. `What if somehow Vileman knows we didn't die at the Schloss.'

`Again, not possible. We have taken great care to stay out of sight, and this place was constructed in total secrecy.'

Wanda shook her head. `Nothing is impossible with those two. And Gunn is in Turkey for one reason only, and we both know it. To suggest his presence is coincidental is the reasoning of an idiot, and you are not an idiot, so do not try to placate me. As I said, we must kill him.'

`What if we do not succeed? What if he really is here by accident? Surely any such action on our part would only arouse his suspicions more. The man has a sixth sense for trouble.'

Wanda mustered all her patience, and replied quietly. `You forget, Maxim Gunn has already seen me, Baron. He knows. There is no room for chance any more.'

The baron was still unhappy. `Better to leave well alone. Turkey is a big place, and we are well-hidden. Only a miracle could lead him here.'

`Gunn has a habit of conjuring miracles,' Wanda replied. `No, we shall arrange a fatal accident. See to it, Baron, and let me know the arrangements. Now, please, leave me. I would like to be alone for a while.'

The Baron inclined his head. `I will see you before you retire tonight - with the plan.'

Wanda Liszt gave no answer. She was already engrossed in her own thoughts. Slowly she became aware of her surroundings again, and was surprised when the wall clock told her an hour had passed. She got up, refilled her glass, and sat back on the settee, lighting a cigarette. She had been reviewing her plans. She picked up a leather covered folder from the table at her side and leafed through the contents. In it were set out the step by step actions she and her lieutenants, the Baron and Auntie de Lorian, were going to undertake.

Until this time her projects had been purely criminal, although of a scope that no-one could have called petty. But since that day when she had suddenly awakened from what had seemed an endless black nothingness, and found herself staring at the shocked faces of the Baron and de Lorian, she had known that nothing could stop her. Coming back to life on the gurney on the instructions of the Professor's programme had been like coming back from the dead, only she had not been dead. Return from death was impossible - and yet, was it? Somehow she had lain in limbo, dormant as a chrysalis waiting for the signal to pupate; a signal that had been supplied by electronic micro impulses.

Between dying and death there was a region of waiting; a cold, dark place where nothing happened and time had no meaning, and something had sought her out and found her there, and become one with her.

It is said there are seven levels of reincarnation, each one to be attained before reaching the ultimate perfection,

Nirvana. So, what happened the other way, she thought? If there were seven levels to perfect enlightenment, should there not also be corresponding levels to ultimate wickedness, to hell. If all forces had equals and opposites, then it was logical. And if there were guides along the path to light, there must also be guides on the path to ultimate darkness. Had one of those guides found her? Did this power she was being given emanate from the touch of an unseen hand? Something stirred in her mind like a cold wind across an ice cap, and she knew the answer was yes.

Something had taken possession of her inner being. It was as if another Wanda Liszt, crueller, more single minded and far less tolerant of the petty doings of her fellow men, had taken up residence in the same body.

Half smiling, she looked across the room and saw her reflection in the large gilt mirror on the far wall. Looking back at her was an incredibly lovely woman. The sapphire dress, accentuating the perfection of her body, highlighted her startling blue eyes, and was even reflected in her dark hair. The overall effect was quite eerie, as though she was surrounded with a strange, glowing light. Was there something there? Another part to her? Had some entity from hell used the paths created by computer logic to become one with her? And was it an ally, or was she merely being used? She threw back her head and laughed, throatily, and decided that she didn't really care. The user, if that was what it was, would become the used. Forces, even the forces of hell, could be controlled. She switched her mind back to the plans and took a sip of her drink.

The plan was simplicity in itself, and mind-numbing in scope. Whatever it was had given her powers, and she intended to use them to make herself mistress of the world.

It was only a short while after her resurrection that she

had discovered just what she had gained, and it had been by accident. The Professor had run a programme in her presence which was linked to the encephalographic graph of one of her guards. He was experimenting with alpha and beta waves to determine whether the specific pattern could be reproduced, as he had a theory that each pattern was as individual as fingerprints; and if so, then instructions could possibly be fed to any person by reproducing their unique pattern and blending it with predetermined instructions in the form of subliminal control. Given the wave pattern, which could be projected from a suitable transmitter, a person could be made to think what was required of them. The wave pattern locked into their brain, and theirs alone, and acted as a carrier for whatever else was pre-programmed.

The guard was the guinea pig, albeit a nervous and unwilling one. Professor Shrinkker took the man's brain pattern, reduced it to computer logic in its component parts, and then fed in a series of simple instructions. Go there. Do that. Say this. He had hooked the man to the computer by electrodes taped to his skull, run the programme - and it had worked. Wanda had been delighted, and had immediately seen the enormous potential.

The first equipment had been clumsy, with the man necessarily linked to the terminal by wires; but finally the Professor had developed a miniaturized transmitter which, either held or worn, or indeed placed within a certain range, had the same effect. Wanda had been like a child with a new and exciting toy. The Professor took wave patterns from the Baron and de Lorian, and she amused herself by controlling them. But the amusement was not innocent; she was not made that way. She could not use it as a party trick, and quickly the cruel side of her new nature emerged. Then she tired of the pettiness, and set about planning.

Money and resources were her first requirements, and

for those she needed a partner with a deep pocket. Her first thought was the Americans. They were quick enough and greedy enough; but she discarded them because she felt they would lack the required ruthless streak. They had a basic humanity that had no place in her plans - and besides, whoever she approached would be accountable in the end to some damned committee.

The British she discarded immediately; not because they lacked the ruthlessness, which she knew they did, but purely and simply because she would not link herself to any group of which Maxim Gunn was a part.

That left the French, the Germans - or the Russians.

The French were too arrogant - though charming, and she liked French men; and the Germans lacked imagination and the ability to improvise in the face of obstacles. They would follow a plan to the death, even if it was wrong.

So she had opted for the hard core Russians, the old school who deeply regretted the passing of Communism, and to that end had made contact.

They had been sceptical, particularly when Shrinkker's name was mentioned, but after the first demonstration on a subject of their choosing, and under controlled conditions, their warm enthusiasm had been gratifying. The funds, and the equipment had been promised the moment she found a suitable centre of operations. And that in itself had presented a problem.

De Lorian and the Baron had taken her apparently lifeless body to Istanbul, where they had a base, and it was a city in which it was easy enough to remain hidden if you had the right contacts, and enough money.

Later they set about searching for a secure place, and there were certain specifications. It had to be away from normal human traffic to make the chance of discovery slight. It had to be big enough to house her staff of guards, and the equipment, in comfort. And it had to be defendable.

Castles were looked at and rejected, partly as a result of the fiasco at the Schloss. She had thought herself secure there, and had been proven wrong. She looked at abandoned mine workings, but rejected them also. They were too new, and the movement that was inevitable would excite curiosity.

In the end, by happy accident, or perhaps, she thought, at the prodding of her alter ego, she had gone to the museum, searched archives, and found mention of the tomb. After that it had taken only a short time to discover that it actually existed and was no legend.

She had installed her people in the vast chambers cut out of the living rock, the equipment had come as promised, and now, after months of work and planning, the small seed had matured into a full-grown plant, and she was nearly ready.

And now there was Maxim Gunn.

She twisted angrily on the settee, and a small growl of suppressed fury and frustration came from between her parted lips.

How? What blighted coincidence had put her on the terrace of the hotel when he had been there? Fate? Or was this presence playing a cat and mouse game with her?

No, she almost shouted as she got up quickly, trying to shake off a feeling of impending disaster. Gunn being there was coincidence, nothing more. And even as she thought it, she knew it was not so. She had seen Gunn, and unspoken words had passed between them. He knew. Somehow he knew, and she had made certain that he would not rest until he had found out by the stupid mistake of trying to kill him in such an amateurish way.

Her powers were great, and getting stronger; but she could not use them to command his death without using his brain patterns, and those, at the moment, were beyond her reach. So, she had to resort to physical means, and she had left the Baron to work out the details.

With a supreme effort she shook all thoughts of Maxim Gunn away, and returned to the substance of her plan. There were last details to perfect before she went to bed, and the Baron would be coming shortly with his plan.

Wanda was lying on the settee, eyes closed, when the Baron returned. In silence she motioned him to a chair, opened her eyes and gazed at him steadily.

`You have the plan I required?' she asked, coldly.

`Naturally, my Lady. It is brief and simple, and cannot fail,' he replied, and proceeded to elaborate on just what was in store for Gunn.

Wanda looked at him thoughtfully for a moment when he finished, and said. `It sounds adequate. They will be out-manoeuvred and out-gunned. Make sure the pilot knows he is to land, and that the others are to personally check the job is satisfactory. I want no mistakes.'

`How can there be mistakes,' said the Baron. `There will be nothing left.'

Wanda sighed, her patience thinning. `Baron. We are not dealing with just anyone; surely you realize this by now. This is Maxim Gunn. Making sure of him is about as difficult as slamming a revolving door.'

The Baron eyed her curiously, and asked. `Is it possible he is undermining your confidence? Sometimes I feel you have too high a regard for his abilities. For what could be luck, maybe you read as skill.'

`Maybe so,' she replied. `And I could wish for that kind of luck on occasion - if it is luck. But I have a feeling this will be the last time. I am a different person now, and so I think is Gunn.' She lit a cigarette and put it in her long, silver holder. `Did you know that even my father was a little afraid of that man?' And seeing the Baron's surprise she smiled. `I must apologize. Gunn has this effect on me. I have been certain he was finished before, and that my plans could be stopped by nothing; and he has made me taste defeat. It is not a diet I relish.'

`This time we shall not fail,' the Baron replied, confidently. `And we shall remove Gunn before he can interfere.'

`Like the bungled attempt in Ankara, I suppose?' Wanda replied, tartly.

The Baron said nothing. He might on occasion disagree with the lady, but never would he criticize her. Wanda stubbed out her cigarette and got gracefully off the settee. The Baron took the hint, wished her good night and left.

CHAPTER SEVEN

Gunn was up at first light before the heat of the day made its all-pervading presence felt, and the only people around were farmers carrying goods to market and the hotel gardeners watering the dusty paths. He ordered breakfast before having a shower, and was towelling himself briskly when the waiter came with his tray; on it was an envelope among the breakfast dishes. He poured some coffee before opening it.

The paper was heavy and expensive, and he raised an eyebrow as he recognized the bold, black, feminine handwriting. What the devil was Wanda Liszt playing at? The note was brief and to the point.

"The price for meddling will be your death."

Nothing like a declaration of war to stir the blood, he thought; but he couldn't understand the woman's game. Surely she knew him better than to imagine that a warning would frighten him off. She obviously had a deeper motive. He shrugged, and tucked the note into Henderson's envelope as there was a thunderous knock at the door.

`Who is it?' he demanded.

`It is I, Tornquist,' came a muted bellow.

Gunn unlocked the door and dragged him in. `For God's sake,' he said. `Keep it down to a dull roar. You'll wake the whole hotel.'

The Swede brushed him aside, almost rudely, and making for his breakfast tray, examined the contents with disgust. Gunn's choice had been figs, rolls and yogurt, which he knew to be first class in Turkey.

`This damned country,' complained Tornquist. `I cannot make them understand that I want breakfast, not this little mess.' And through a large mouthful, he begged. `Order for me, my friend. A man like me, of my size, needs proper food.'

Gunn was unsympathetic. `Do you good to get away from the pickled herrings and cheese - and that's mine.'

Tornquist sighed massively. `And I thought the English and Swedes were allies.'

Gunn ignored the remark. `Since you're here, you'd better sit back and listen. We've got to make a plan.'

Tornquist snorted derisively. `What plan is needed? All we do is find these people, break up their pretty things, and take this woman - Wanda? - back for the police to deal with.'

Gunn sighed wearily. `Don't you ever listen to anything, you great hairy Viking? I repeat, these people are dangerous, very dangerous, and wading in with your battle axe waving around your head would simply be a quick way of committing suicide. For some reason, this time she is totally confident.' He explained the note. `Anyway, handing them over to the law won't solve anything. They've got to be finished; finally and forever.'

`Like, how you say, terminated?'

`Yes. Terminated,' replied Gunn.

`So,' Tornquist laughed. `That saves much trouble. No need to bring them back. It is easier.'

`Yes,' agreed Gunn, dryly. `Much trouble. But we're going to have much trouble in the meantime.'

Tornquist retained his affable smile, and Gunn started to have serious reservations about the man's involvement.

`First,' Gunn continued, `You gather all the information you can on the area, anything at all: photos, maps, geological data, anything that might give us a clue as to where this mythical cavern of yours might be.'

`This I already have,' replied Tornquist. `You think I

have been searching blind all these years.'

`Then why haven't you found it?' asked Gunn.

`Because I have been doing the looking alone, and it is a very big area.'

`And this time it's going to be different?'

`Of course,' said Tornquist, firmly.

`Why?'

`For such an intelligent man,' Tornquist replied, with a sad look, `You can be stupid. This time the woman helps us. She has already thrown a challenge, which she knows you will accept, and somewhere along the way she will try to get rid of you, again. But we will be expecting that. We will not have to find her I think; she will lead us, into a trap. And we will obligingly fall into it.'

`And then we have her,' said Gunn, with a smile. `Once she has us tied up and under sentence of death, we have her exactly where we want her, eh?'

`Exactly. Simple, no?'

`Alarmingly so. On second thoughts I don't think we'll plan. I think we'll play it by ear. In the meantime, I have an appointment and there are one or two things you can organize.'

Ten minutes later Gunn was on his way to his meeting with Rostov, having given Tornquist a list of things to do.

The taxi took off like a rocket down the Ataturk Boulevard, and Gunn sat back philosophically as they scorched in the direction of the Citadel and its warren of old and narrow lanes, wondering what Rostov was going to be like.

For a split second Gunn thought it had been a backfire, and then the shattered side window of the taxi lying in a heap of diamond shards around him, told him it had been a shot - and no ordinary one at that.

The entire window beside him had been blown clean out and the one on the opposite side smashed. Only his action of slumping back in the seat had saved his head being taken with it.

The driver whirled round with a look of open-mouthed outrage and shock, and then slammed on his brakes, screeched to a halt and jumped out. Gunn, by that time, was on the floor with the nearside door half open, and half a second later was on the sidewalk, crouched behind a tree.

Either shotgun blasts, and double-barrelled at that, and passengers baling out of taxis were common sights in Ankara, or no-one had even noticed what had happened amid the general city noise.

Gunn watched as a black Mercedes took off into the traffic and vanished round a corner with a squeal of tires. He got up and dusted off his trousers. This was getting a bit distracting. Two attempts on his life in twelve hours. Wanda obviously meant business, and maybe Tornquist was right about her power being limited; or maybe she needed the computer for those. He felt himself getting increasingly confused about the whole deal of black magic and unseen whatevers. He decided to make a special effort to avoid the third attempt - it might be the lucky one.

The driver had disappeared, but whether he was part of the plot or just plain scared, Gunn didn't know, and didn't greatly care. He hailed another taxi that was dropping its fare, and a few minutes later got out in front of an iron-studded door set in a blank wall.

He looked carefully about before pulling the bell chain which hung from a bracket. There was no obvious ringing and he assumed it was connected to the back of the house. Presently he heard the slap of sandals on a stone floor, and a small peep hole slid back to reveal a pair of dark, suspicious eyes. He introduced himself in Russian as his knowledge of Turkish was slight. The peephole slid shut, and with a thunk the main door bolts were drawn and it swung open, revealing a darkened courtyard. The doorkeeper motioned him to follow, and they crossed the courtyard to another door.

Gunn found himself in a small, poorly furnished room, with small windows letting in little of the morning sun. There was a smell of cooking, and of things that were not too clean.

`Please be seated, Mr Gunn,' said a rusty voice, and turning he made out a shadowy figure which had emerged from behind a curtain in one corner.

`Mr Rostov?' Gunn asked.

`The same. It was good of you to be so punctual.'

`Termaxian said a visit would be worth my while. I saw little point in ignoring his advice,' replied Gunn.

Rostov smiled without humour. `You speak Russian without a trace of accent. I must compliment you.'

`I had good teachers.'

Again he was treated to the humourless smile. `Quite so. But you did not come here to discuss such things, I imagine. Termaxian has told me nothing, of course; but he expressed a desire that I should place my resources at your disposal.'

It took Gunn only a short while to explain to Rostov as much as he felt he should know. Wanda Liszt and the Baron were familiar names to him, and at the mention of the outlaw power involvement he suddenly became very co-operative. If it had not been for Termaxian's recommendation, Gunn would have trusted him about as far as he could have thrown a bull elephant. His whole appearance was one of shifty deceit, but there was no denying his ability and knowledge.

`I will do what I can to help you, Mr Gunn,' he said at length. `There is a man in Adana who will be expecting you and will help further, if necessary. The weapons you require are no problem and will be delivered once you are on your way. A man will stop you once you are clear of the city. It is best that way as we do not know how well you are being watched.' Gunn smiled at that; it appeared he was being watched very closely. `Will that suit?'

Gunn nodded. `Who is this man of yours in Adana?'

`His name is Mahmut Kamal, and he will contact you. Stay at the Buyuk Surmeli hotel. It is the best there is. And now, with your permission I must be about our business. Some things take a little time to arrange.'

`And the matter of payment?' asked Gunn.

Rostov spread his hands. `That is taken care of. Termaxian has put certain valuable information in my hands. It is enough.'

Gunn nodded and rose. `You have no idea who the people might be who tried to cut short my career last night, and again this morning?'

Rostov shrugged. `Every big city has its share of thugs for hire, Mr Gunn. Just don't walk under any ladders. But if you like I will make inquiries.'

Gunn was about to make some mention of the more peculiar aspects of the matter; Wanda Liszt's supposed familiarity with the darker side of things, but he changed his mind. Rostov was doing what he wanted, and treating him as a perfectly sane human being who needed a few illicit items. But bring black magic, however rationalized by computer technology, into the conversation and he might renege, Termaxian or not.

Gunn shook his head. `Don't bother. You've been more than helpful.' He paused. `Actually, there is one thing I do need. Airport security being what it is these days, I was unable to bring in a hand gun.'

Rostov smiled toothily and reached inside his jacket. `I had anticipated as much.' He produced a Colt Python. `Will this do?'

Gunn quickly examined the powerful weapon. `It will

do very nicely. Thank you, and good-bye.'

Rostov led him through the courtyard, and as he saw him out, said. `Do not return here, Mr Gunn. Madame Liszt has a way of finding things out, and I prefer not to come to her attention. If you need anything further, tell the man who will meet you on the road tomorrow, or Mahmut Kamal.'

Gunn spent the rest of the day about his own business. A visit to the Anatolian Museum provided him with a valuable insight into the history of the Bolkar Dag area and the Taurus mountains, and a pleasant lunch at the Jockey Club gave him some information that caused his eyes to harden at the mention of a well-known name. He also got a valuable tip for a race later that day and collected on a rank outsider.

The evening shadows were lengthening as he strolled back to his hotel through the park and down the wide, tree lined boulevard. The fierce heat of the day was gone, giving way to a warm, scented dusk.

Back in his room, he showered the heat and dust of the day off, and was sitting at ease, dressed in a towelling robe with a Glenmorangie in his hand, when the telephone rang. He reached out a hand and winced as the giant Swede's voice boomed out at him, saying he'd be right along. Gunn asked him mildly why he bothered about such things as telephones, when a simple bellow would have let most of Ankara know. He sighed, cradled the hand piece, and went to put on his clothes.

CHAPTER EIGHT

Deep inside the mountain, many yards from the cliff face, in chambers that had once been the tomb of the great Gilgamesh, king of Uruk who reigned around 2600 B.C., was the operational headquarters of WORM, the acronym that stood for the World Organization for the Re-education of Mankind. It was an innocent sounding title that belied a deadly purpose.

In the drawing room, the Baron and Wanda Liszt were discussing the plans of the current venture.

`My dear Baron,' she said. `As you know, this is by far our most ambitious scheme, and we must make sure that even more than our customary care is taken. We have a bedfellow this time whose cunning is almost a match for my own.'

`A cunning bedfellow we can put up with,' replied the Baron. `And no doubt kick out of bed when the time comes. The fly in the ointment is Maxim Gunn, and soon he will be disposed of.'

Wanda shifted uneasily in her chair and lit a cigarette.

`I hope you are right,' she said. `The man's uncanny ability to survive bothers me.'

The Baron swirled brandy in his glass, sniffed it and gave her an amused look over the rim. `Really, my Lady. There have been times when I have almost been able to persuade myself that you were more than a little in love with him. It is said that the borderline between love and hate is very fine.'

Wanda's reaction was sharp, and angry, and he instantly regretted the remarks. `Do not even joke about such things,' she spat. `Gunn's name is anathema to me, and all I require of you is to see that he is terminated.' For a moment longer she glared at him, and then got up with a lithe, sinewy movement, crossed to a glass-topped table and picked up the leather-covered folder.

`In here, as you know, are the plans for the takeover of all key political, military and industrial personnel, world-wide. Let me refresh your memory.'

The Baron, glad that the moment had passed, sat back more comfortably and blew a smoke ring at the ceiling, marvelling yet again that anyone so young and totally beautiful could have a mind capable of not only formulating the devastation plans that seemed to come so easily to her, but the ruthlessness to carry them out. She was indeed her father's daughter, and had been taught well. It also seemed, he was reminded uncomfortably, that she had become something else. Wanda Liszt ran a hand over her smooth, dark hair and flicked through the pages of the dossier.

`Stage one is the demonstration we are going to carry out for our partners, to prove finally that the system works beyond doubt.'

`Surely they know it works, we have shown them,' said the Baron.

`Please do not interrupt,' replied Wanda, coldly. `I have arranged to be one of the acts at a special charity performance of conjuring and such like, to be held at the Palladium Theatre in London next month. I shall be billed as Madame Danwa, the Oriental Mystic and mind reader. The guest of honour is to be the British Prime Minister. During the performance I shall give him orders for the release of two men recently convicted of terrorism, and being held at Wormwood Scrubs prison. There is no value to our partners in their release as such. It is purely the final demonstration.'

`The men being Ahmed Hassan and Abdul Malik.'

Wanda scowled at the further interruption, and then

shrugged. `Correct.'

`And what of the WORM bugs?' asked the Baron.

Wanda pulled a face. `An unfortunate name for such an ingenious device - so trite. Be that as it may; these little miracles which the Professor has devised will be planted in the immediate vicinity of certain of the world's most influential people. The Prime Minister's will be in the arm of his seat - we have already obtained his brain pattern - and it amazes me how easy these patterns are to obtain.'

`The medical ...'

`... check ups, yes. For people who are normally so security conscious, and indeed ringed by security, they are inordinately lax when in a doctor's office.'

`Everyone trusts their doctor, even security men, and such people pay very regular visits. It goes with the job, so to speak.'

`The doctors knew nothing, as you are aware. If you can bug a telephone - which is checked, how easy is it to use one of ours, which is not, because its existence is not suspected.'

`And now we have the brain patterns of everyone we need?' the Baron asked.

Wanda nodded. `The prime targets. Others will be obtained as we need them.' And then seeing that the Baron had a question he was hesitant about asking. `Yes?'

`Our brain patterns,' he replied. `De Lorian's and mine. Can these not now be removed from the records? Surely you will not need them now the experimental stage is over?'

Wanda threw back her head and laughed, but there was no humour in it. The sound gave the Baron an uncomfortable chill.

`Oh no,' she said, firmly. `You two may be my lieutenants, and I trust you of course. But let me just call it insurance. No, the patterns stay.'

There was a time when the Baron would have argued, even insisted; but the re-born Wanda frightened him. With a wry smile and a shrug, he said. `As you wish, my Lady.'

Wanda nodded. `Anyway, to business. The key people at the moment are: the President of the United States, the Pope, the President of France, the Premier of Japan ...' She made a throw-away gesture and flicked over a couple of pages. `But we needn't go into all that. Once we have them "thinking" our way we can move in on the major industrial empires - General Motors, Exxon, Dupont, Shell, Mitsui, etcetera, including the financial and mining cartels.' She placed her chin on her hand and smiled with inner amusement. `It would be a great entertainment to try this on the United Nations during a full sitting.'

The Baron laughed. `To have all the delegates agreeing on something at the same time would be a unique experience. But tell me, is there no way to broadcast the pattern worldwide in some way, and achieve immediate takeover?'

Wanda shook her head. `The brain patterns, Baron. How do you get over five billion brain patterns? And if you could, what kind of computer and beaming mechanism would you need? Impossible, and anyway, we do not want the people, we want the leaders. Once we have them the people can be brought to their knees. We want slaves, not zombies.'

`Worms - if you'll pardon the pun - can turn,' replied the Baron.

Wanda shrugged. `Even worms need leaders, and as one emerges we shall simply remove the influence.'

The Baron sighed, and tapped a length of ash from his cigar.

`I don't suppose I shall ever understand how Shrinkker's device works, other than the fact that it generates thought impulses linked to the brain pattern.'

`You don't need to,' Wanda replied. `And anyway, Shrinkker's device is only part of it. The rest is here.' And she tapped her breast. There is more power in here than you dream of, Baron, and it is not from computers - or even this earth.'

The Baron was silent. He did not trust himself to reply. The woman before him was changed - that he knew, but he did not understand what she had just said. He had only his suspicions.

`No,' said Wanda, briskly. `Once we have the British Prime Minister under our control, you will undertake your mission to Washington. An appointment has been sought, and granted, with the President. You are to be the European representative of WORM, and as such merely wish to make our peaceful and most praiseworthy objectives known to him. The meeting will be brief, and whilst in the Oval Office, you will present him with a small token of our esteem; one of our beautiful fountain pens. He will accept it as it is too lovely and valuable not to, and will no doubt carry it on his person.' She paused to take a sip of her drink. `After all, we are an organization dedicated to the re-education of mankind; dedicated to peace, to the stamping out of war and the old prejudices of colour, creed and ethnic origin.' She laughed softly. `What world leader would not want to be associated with those aims - in public, at least. Anyway, it is true, those are our aims. When we have taken over those things will simply cease to exist. I think we may safely say we have the interests of all men at heart.'

`So,' said the Baron. `Stage one begins on the fifth - in fact the day after tomorrow.' He rubbed his hands together quickly. `I can feel the excitement and anticipation mounting, my Lady. When do you intend to leave?'

`Tomorrow. There is no need to be in London before. I have no equipment or stage rehearsal to do - just the one small box which is already prepared. The seat the Prime

Minister will occupy is already known and it will be a simple matter to install.'

`And the man will be ours.'

Wanda nodded her satisfaction. `As you say, he will be ours, and without being aware of it - as soon as he receives his gift. The man is known for his iron will. Maybe we shall melt a little of that iron.'

`And then we make a start on the changes in Britain,' the Baron enthused.

`And then we do nothing,' Wanda replied, sharply. `Other than that which we have already discussed. To proceed at too rapid a pace would almost certainly create suspicion. This must be done subtly.'

The Baron replied, hesitantly. `It would seem there are already suspicions.'

Wanda Liszt whirled on him. `Gunn?'

The Baron nodded. `And Vileman.'

Wanda jabbed a finger at him. `Gunn you are taking care of, and without him Vileman will be powerless until it is too late. See that there are no mistakes in your plan, Baron. Gunn is already close enough.' She lit a cigarette and threw herself back against the settee, scowling, and the Baron knew their talk was finished. Without a word, he got up and quietly left the chamber.

For a long time after the Baron had left, Wanda Liszt remained motionless, smoking one cigarette after another without being aware of her actions. Despite her new found powers, Maxim Gunn worried her more than she was prepared to admit, even to her closest associates. There was an indestructibility about the man that went far beyond the normal, and her mind's eye unwillingly conjured up the image of his darkly handsome face with the permanent hint of amusement in the clear, blue eyes.

Her powers were growing - she felt it - but as yet they were not enough to deal with him by them alone. The dependence on violent and physical methods irritated her, but she knew she had to be satisfied - for the time. Gracefully she got to her feet and stared once again at her reflection in the long mirror, analyzing what she saw. There was great beauty, but she was used to that, and there had always been strength in the proud tilt of her head and clear, dark eyes. But there was definitely something else - that new dimension to her mind, and it too looked out from the same eyes.

If he had not been expecting it, the thunderous knocking on the door might have made Gunn think he was being invaded by Mongol hordes. As it was he quickly opened it before the paint work could be damaged and the management present him with a repair bill.

`God knows how you manage to archaeologize anything,' he said to Tornquist. `One touch from you would wreck anything the past may have had to offer. I bet you don't even bother with a bulldozer, or explosives. You probably just kick the ground away.'

`My friend,' the Swede boomed. `I am as gentle as a baby just now. You should see me when I am angry.'

`I'll save that pleasure for when it's needed,' replied Gunn, dryly. `Come in anyway and tell me what you've been doing.'

Tornquist's eyes lit up at the sight of the bottle of Glenmorangie, and he loped in like a friendly grizzly bear, dumping a roll of maps on the table.

`I have spent all day with the Departments of Antiquities and Geology,' he said, as he poured a stiff measure of whisky and gulped it down. `And I think I get the search narrowed down to a few possible places,' and reaching for the maps he unrolled them, weighting the corners with glasses. `Come, look and I show you.'

For the next hour the two men poured over the data, and then Gunn sat back feeling a little more hopeful.

`You know,' he said. `If you are right, you are going to

rank along with Schliemann and Howard Carter as a discoverer.'

The Swede frowned. `Bah. Theirs was nothing. They only found what everyone knew had to be there. I shall have found the impossible.'

Gunn smiled at the man's ego. `I'm still puzzled as to why you didn't find it years ago, if all it took was an afternoon in a museum to narrow down the likely spots.'

Tornquist shrugged. `Perhaps I needed a push. Also perhaps I am completely wrong.' He gave a bellow of laughter. `No. I am never wrong. We will find this Wanda of yours, and break her in little pieces. But seriously my friend, I think we should try these two places first. They are most likely, and the topography fits with the cliffs.' He scratched his beard and looked at Gunn with a wry smile. `I wonder why I did not think of cliffs before, it is so obvious.'

`We all have twenty-twenty hindsight,' Gunn replied.

`Even you?' asked Tornquist with a twinkle in his eye.

Gunn chose to ignore him. `You had no trouble with the equipment?'

`No. We can start at any time. The sooner the better I think.'

`Good. Then let's get some dinner and have an early night. We'll leave at dawn.'

Tornquist heaved himself to his feet. `Good. My stomach begins to think my throat has been cut.'

After dinner Gunn returned to his room and placed a call through to Vileman's office, attaching a small scrambler to the instrument before he did so.

Vileman came through loud and clear, and Gunn thought he and Tornquist would get on well together. They'd be able to dispense with such trivial things as phones over a mere thousand miles or so.

In a few crisp sentences he explained the situation,

allayed Vileman's worries about bringing an outsider into the business, and rejected an offer for more manpower. Then he arranged to call again from Adana, and hung up.

As he had a last drink before turning in, Gunn thought briefly about the next day. He would have preferred to fly south, but he needed Tornquist and his equipment, and he wasn't at all sure there would be time to set it up in Adana. So, there was nothing for it but to drive the two hundred and fifty miles over the high Anatolian plateau. He wished he had time to play the tourist, as with Tornquist as a guide he would have learned so much. As it was it would be a quick dash, and then the hard slog of searching through the Taurus mountains.

As he got into bed and switched off the light, he gave a fleeting thought to the Gods of battle and luck. He was going to need their goodwill if this thing was going to be pulled off.

CHAPTER NINE

It was dark when Gunn and Tornquist drove out of the hotel garage, down Ataturk Boulevard, and turned south on the E5 highway. It was still too early for even the most unfortunate workers to be about, and they had the road to themselves. Within minutes they were out of the city and speeding through the still country. Gunn was driving the first stretch as he was expecting to be stopped to take on the additional equipment. He also knew that if another attempt was going to be made in the Ankara area, this was when it could happen, in the quiet dawn countryside.

As they approached a small village, in which a few lamps shone in the windows of early risers, Gunn slowed down, thinking it was the right place for Rostov's messenger. There was no sign as he cruised slowly down the dusty street between the trees, but he had a feeling they were being watched; and sure enough, just as they left the last house behind, a torch flashed on and off, and then jiggled up and down. Gunn slowed to a stop and pulled in to the side, all senses alert and his hand on the butt of the Colt Python. He felt Tornquist tense at his side and murmured. `Relax. Leave this to me.'

Two men came out of the darkness, one from each side of the road, and Gunn's sixth sense told him there were others beyond his field of vision. They were careful men, and he respected them for it. They wouldn't have lasted long in their business by being stupid.

The man at Tornquist's window spoke in passable English. `Which is Maxim Gunn?'

Gunn raised his hand off the wheel in acknowledgement, and the man went on. `We have things for you.

Please open the back of the car.'

Gunn got out and did as asked, and three shadows moved out of the bushes at the side of the road. Moments later a couple of bundles were loaded, and the men disappeared as silently as they had come. As the leader reached the edge of darkness, he paused and raised his hand, and Gunn heard the words. `Allah Ismarladik. Go with God.' He smiled grimly, raised his hand in reply, and two minutes later they were speeding on their way and the first grey light of dawn was spreading across the eastern horizon.

The two men were silent for a long time, each wrapped in his own thoughts. Gunn wondered how, and when, Wanda was going to make her presence felt. The attempts on his life in Ankara had been amateurish, and probably more in the way of wild stabs than anything. Somehow he felt that she would stay her hand until later, until he began to get closer to the trap she was setting - for a trap it had to be. Wanda was not a bungler - but the Baron?

Somewhere along the way she would make a direct frontal attack in an all out effort to wipe him out. So, he thought, when you're walking into the lion's den, nice and easy does it. No sense in rattling the bars to let him know you're coming.

The fact that he wasn't bothered about the outcome of such an attack was an indication of Maxim Gunn's superb faith in his own ability. There were risks, to be sure, and he accepted them as part of his way of life, but somehow he knew he would be in at the end.

He turned to Tornquist, and said. `We'll stop for coffee when the sun gets up.'

`And breakfast,' grumbled the Swede. `If I don't get food my brain will cease to work, and you will spend the rest of your life wandering like the prophet in the wilderness.'

`If I thought starvation would stop your mouth working,' Gunn replied, `I'd drive on forever.'

In the cavern complex deep in the Taurus Mountains, Wanda Liszt, the Baron and Auntie de Lorian were enjoying a much better breakfast than Gunn and Tornquist, when a messenger from the wireless room knocked and entered with news that Gunn had left the hotel in Ankara and was heading south. Wanda listened and dismissed the man.

`It seems you will be able to put your plan into action, Baron. Gunn is on his way. It will be easy to trail him from here on, so see it is done. When the time is right, strike, and let there be no mistakes.' She poured another cup of coffee and lit a cigarette. `One thing puzzles me though. Gunn usually works alone - though we must remember Siriani - so, who is this Tornquist?'

Auntie de Lorian leaned back in her chair and replied. `I was curious about that, so I made inquiries. Torquil Tornquist is a well-known archaeologist. He is immensely rich, and has devoted his life to the study of Hittite and Phrygian civilizations. I regret to say he has also shown great promise as a student of the Gilgamesh Tablets. Gunn has obviously brought him along as a resident expert.'

`How can Gunn possibly know about that?' Wanda snapped.

`I do not know, but I mistrust coincidences.'

`You mean this Tornquist fellow might be able to trace these caverns?' asked the Baron.

`That is doubtful. Too little is known about Gilgamesh. And yet...'

`And yet you think he might point Gunn in the right direction,' said Wanda.

`Yes, my dear,' replied the older woman. `It seems Tornquist may have found some fresh evidence. He has been generally laughed at, but it could make him a dangerous ally.'

`You should have told me this before,' said Wanda. `Now, more than ever, Baron, it becomes imperative that you carry out your plan. How did Gunn meet this man?'

`While ejecting a thief from his hotel room it seems.'

Wanda whirled. `I told you, Baron. The man has the luck of the devil. My father was right to fear him I think.'

Back in London, Indigo Boone, Vileman's Chief of Staff, was slumped in a chair, surrounded by a blue grey haze of pipe smoke. Neither had been able to start the day and get on with normal work, and they were both worried. Vileman had just been voicing his fears to the phlegmatic Yorkshireman. Boone leaned forward and knocked the dottle out of his pipe.

`No, Chief,' he said. `My only worry is that Gunn won't get the timing right. He might get there too late to stop the damned woman. We don't know where they are, and Turkey's a big place. This ancient cavern idea sounds a bit far-fetched, but what else have we to go on? No, I'm not worried about the man, he'll be all right. Lord, he could land feet first in a nest of cobras, and all he'd get would be a new pair of snakeskin shoes.'

Vileman growled, but whether in agreement or disbelief was hard to tell.

`Why don't they just plug their damned machine into the Telly or something?' he asked.

`Wouldn't work,' replied Boone. `Most of the programmes are canned, and practically nothing goes out that isn't delayed transmission at least, just in case something embarrassing happens. And that wipes out the effect apparently.'

`Well, thank God for that. T.V.'s enough to turn you mindless as it is, without someone trying to do it deliberately.'

`He said he'd contact again from Adana,' said Boone, and got up stiffly. `I think I'll go to my office and catch up with what's been coming in.'

`Catch up with the cricket scores more likely,' replied Vileman with a wry smile. `How are we doing?'

`Got 'em on the run. What the Aussies need is a miracle.'

`They have my sympathy. We need a miracle too.'

It was mid-afternoon when the two men arrived in Adana. Apart from a brief spell with Tornquist at the wheel, during which time Gunn had endured agonies as they missed an assortment of animals and other vehicles by less than the thickness of a coat of paint, he had driven all the way.

They checked into the hotel and went to freshen up. Gunn decided he would go into the empty country outside town later, to check and sight the rifles so silently delivered in the dawn hours. There was nothing else to do in the meantime, and he drove out to the Seyhan dam for a swim and to clear his mind.

After dinner that evening he sighted the rifles, much to the surprise of a couple of sleepy goatherds, then returned to the hotel, planning another early night and an even earlier start, and it was then that the Gods of Luck gave him a wink of encouragement.

He had picked up a day-old London paper from the porter's desk and was glancing through the headlines as he removed his shirt, when an item caught his eye. It was to the effect that there was to be a charity performance at the Palladium Theatre, at which the Prime Minister was the guest of honour. Something made him read it, and he was just kicking off his shoes when the name of one of the acts leapt off the page at him. "*Mind reading and Mesmerism, by Madame Danwa.*" He stared at the name, transfixed, and then swore horribly. Christ! For Danwa, read WANDA! and the P.M. would be there. It was no coincidence, and Wanda Liszt did not let her face be seen in public without good reason.

In two strides he reached the phone and asked reception for a London number, then took out the Glenmorangie, poured himself a stiff drink and downed it in one gulp. He glanced at his watch and tapped the empty glass impatiently. Come on. Come on! For God's sake. The performance was tonight, and with the time difference, the curtain would go up in an hour.

He was about to pour another drink when the phone rang. He snatched it up, and curtly shut Vileman off in mid-question. In a few clipped words he explained the situation, explained his plans, and the moment Vileman acknowledged, hung up to avoid wasting a second. He straightened, sighed and poured the drink, satisfied that the Prime Minister would not be attending the show. The Iron Prime Minister might indeed have a corresponding will, but when Vileman advised, he acted. That much he knew.

Ten minutes later he was in bed, and asleep the moment his head touched the pillow.

CHAPTER TEN

They had started while the stars were still bright in the sky, and throughout the long day had worked their way up into the mountains, over passes and onto little travelled tracks. The only signs of life had been the occasional goat herd and, twice, a small village nestling in the shelter of the stony hills.

It was nearly sunset when Gunn called a halt under a group of stunted trees beneath a hill covered with tumbled boulders. The gear unpacked, he lit a small fire of thorn wood, and within a short time had applied his not inconsiderable talents to dinner. The result would have satisfied the most demanding gourmet.

Leaning back against a boulder, a mug of wine in his hand and a cigar between his teeth, Torquil Tornquist uttered a sigh of contentment, and said. `A wise man once inferred that any fool could be uncomfortable when camping. You, my friend, are obviously not a fool. The dinner was superb, the wine has travelled remarkably well, and this cigar - which is obviously Cuban, and therefore illegal - is magnificent.'

Gunn grunted and waved a hand in airy acknowledgement. `Tell me about this Gilgamesh character. My knowledge of him is sketchy, to say the least. Wasn't he supposed to have been a visitor from another planet who became a God King, and reigned for an impossible number of years?'

Tornquist chuckled. `One hundred and twenty-six to be precise. But as to the rest - who knows. Listen, and I will tell you what is known, and what I think.'

Bright stars shone through the clear, dry air, and nothing but the sigh of the wind, and the occasional cry of a night creature disturbed Tornquist's tale of an ancient king, lord of one of the city states of the so-called cradle of civilization. He recited parts of the Epic of Gilgamesh, and in his enthusiasm transformed it from dusty, far off history, to the deeds of a man who was truly great in his time. It was a story of violence and love, friendship and high adventure - and of death, and Gunn was moved by it, by a man who had lived some 4,600 years ago - and was still remembered. He wondered vaguely how many people living today would be remembered in the year 6,500 - not many - if there were indeed men to remember, if the world hadn't destroyed itself by then.

`So the tablets are incomplete,' he said when Tornquist finally came to the end. `We don't know what happened to him in the final days.'

`Not officially,' replied the archaeologist. `But I think I know, and that is why we are here in this God forsaken place. Why he came here to end his days we shall never know. Maybe it wasn't so bleak then. Maybe there were trees and pasture where there is now rock and bareness.' He shrugged. `Anyway, we shall see.'

In the distance, to the north, Gunn watched with mild curiosity as the navigation lights of an aircraft winked through the night, and the faint beat told him it was a helicopter. It was more than twenty-four hours since his urgent call to Vileman, and he was blissfully unaware that the craft contained Wanda Liszt, returning to her lair, furious at the failure of her mission in London.

Tornquist built up the fire as the desert night would soon turn cold, and the men turned in, both with a strange sense of being on the brink of something. Tornquist sensed the coming fulfilment of his long quest, and Gunn, absently fingering the amulet which lay against his chest, felt an instinct that his real mission was about to start. The image of Wanda Liszt, darkly beautiful and contrasting sharply with her white gown, floated before his closed eyes. He had read the message in those eyes on the terrace of the hotel, and knew that while he was not much closer to finding her than he had been in London, she would find him. If she had occupied Tornquist's lost tomb, and if they were in fact going in the right direction, he knew she would try to finish it before he got much closer.

For a few moments he wondered about the powers Vileman and old Termaxian had talked of. Fact, or stories told in the dark to frighten? Did she really have something? Had she really harnessed an ally that was not of the normal world? Mentally he shrugged. There was no knowing. He would find out soon enough. Almost superstitiously he touched the amulet, and drew a strange comfort from it. And then, with a sharp feeling of anger at himself for behaving in such a way, he rolled on his side and was asleep in moments.

Wanda Liszt swept into the luxurious living quarters in the caverns. The fact that it had been the main burial chamber within the tomb complex, and had a subtle atmosphere, appealed to her sense of the macabre. At that moment, however, she was experiencing nothing but overwhelming anger. She was wild with disappointment at the failure of her mission, and as yet unable to fathom how the failure had occurred. Reason told her that the Prime Minister's sudden cancellation was pure coincidence, but her instincts screamed that Maxim Gunn was at the bottom of it. God, how she hated the man.

She drew off long gloves and discarded the full-length ocelot coat she had worn against the cold of the flight, the red silk lining flashing vividly in the subdued lamplight, and slumped angrily on the settee. The Baron, quick to sense something was wrong, poured brandy for them both, and spoke briefly into a telephone.

Wanda Liszt nursed the balloon glass, seemingly unaware of his presence and lost in thought until there was a gentle knock on the door. The Baron crossed the room and opened it and a man in para-military uniform entered. Wanda turned, head thrown back, poised and beautiful.

`Everything is ready?' she asked, coldly. `The instructions have been carried out?'

`Yes, my Lady. We are waiting for your final orders.'

Wanda passed her glass to the attentive Baron. `Make the attack at dawn, tomorrow. They will be least expecting anything then.'

The man hesitated and she snapped. `What is it?'

`The target, my Lady. We have no position.'

Wanda closed her eyes and breathed deeply. `I will give you that, later. Now go.' She accepted the refilled glass from the Baron as the man left and drank deeply as if needing it. `The Prime Minister cancelled,' she said, savagely.

The Baron's eyebrows shot up, startled. `You mean ..'

`Yes. Dammit. The whole thing was abortive - a waste of time and effort. And I had to stand in front of those fools for half an hour, doing party tricks. It was humiliating, Baron. I, Wanda Liszt, a common entertainer for a thousand overfed, sycophantic fools. And before you say anything, no, I could not have cancelled my performance.' She put stress and contempt into the word. `The announcement came at the last moment, and to have walked out might have caused suspicion.'

`Was a reason given?'

Wanda shrugged. `Some nonsense about a crisis situation. It doesn't matter. What matters is that he was not there, and I have been made to look incompetent before our partners.'

`You could not have foreseen it,' replied the Baron, soothingly. `Things happen to the best plans. We shall have to try again. There are other ways.'

Wanda gave him a withering look and said slowly and

distinctly, her voice throaty with suppressed emotion. `It did not just happen, Baron. I feel it here.' She pressed her hand against her breast. `Somehow Maxim Gunn is behind this. I know it.'

The Baron was incredulous. `My Lady. That is not possible. Gunn is more than a thousand miles from London. He is here, in the mountains. You know that. How could he possibly ...?'

`I don't know how,' she snarled. `I just know that he did. Now please leave me. I have work to do. I must find him.'

Wanda Liszt had discovered two things about her new powers. The first was that they worked, which in itself was sufficient. The second was that she had to create an aura of mystery around it, mystery as great as the powers themselves, and to that end she indulged in a fair amount of play-acting.

Her company, the Baron and Auntie de Lorian included, knew there was something beyond their understanding, and were content to let it go at that, not wishing to become involved. Hard, practical criminals they both were, but like many of their kind they had a strong mistrust of the unexplainable. They dealt in facts: actions and reactions, and their tools were blackmail, bribery, violence and extortion. Magic, with all its implications left them unaccountably uncomfortable. Professor Edouard Shrinkker on the other hand had no such reservations. His brilliant mind had created the programmes by which Wanda's dying brain had been revived; and what he created he understood. What he did not understand was that she had come back from the brink of death a different person, with an understanding and control - mind over matter - that he found fascinating. It was his intention to probe until he too found the secret.

Thus it was that when Wanda emerged from her

chambers some time later, curiously dressed in a long, flowing dark cape worked with recognizable cabalistic symbols, and making for the computer room, she was avoided by everyone. The men she passed barely acknowledged her passing, and became suddenly engrossed in whatever they were doing. The Baron and de Lorian were nowhere to be seen.

Wanda swept theatrically along the rock cut tunnels, head high and with her gaze trance-like, until she came to the pressure doors of the clean room and swept inside. Immediately she dropped her pose and became practical. The Professor looked up from his work and saw her, and her dress.

`Ah,' he exclaimed, in a satisfied voice. `More experiments?'

Wanda stopped, gave him a hard look and shook her head. `No experiments. This time I have work. I shall be scrying.'

The Professor was interested immediately. `There is something you wish to know?'

`Someone I want to find,' Wanda replied. From the tone of her voice Shrinkker decided he was glad he was not that person.

`I will set up the equipment,' he said, and hurried off, chuckling and shaking his head in wonder; and well he might. Prior to his current employment, Professor Shrinkker's only familiarity with scrying had been in the booths at fair grounds when he was a boy in his native Austria, and it had involved unlikely women, who professed to be fortune tellers, gazing into cheap glass balls and coming up with answers for the price of a few *schilling*. Even at that age he had quickly decided the whole thing was a fake. And that opinion remained - until he started work with Wanda Liszt. She did not use a crystal ball, but the effect was the same as the fairground gypsies intended, but with a difference: it worked.

At the far end of the room the walls and floor had been bizarrely decorated. Dark velvet hangings, worked with similar designs to those on her robe, hung from roof to floor; and on the floor was a pentagram, a five pointed star, made of silver and set into black marble tiles. Around the pentagram was a circular collar divided into twelve segments, each containing a sign of the zodiac. It was to this point, the centre of the pentagram, that he wheeled a thoroughly modern computer terminal and display unit. He plugged it into a jack in the floor, switched it on, and left the area. The zodiacal signs he knew were just so much decoration, but the pentagram itself intrigued him. In the folklore of demonology it was the protective barrier within which the sorcerer stood, safe from the demons he summoned, and he had enough of an inquiring mind, and enough pragmatism, to realize that behind almost every myth and ritual there was a basis of truth, however distorted by time. Maybe the shape created a force field of some kind ...

He was interrupted in his musings by Wanda Liszt, impatient to start. `Is it ready?' she demanded. Shrinkker nodded and pointed to the screen, already lit up and showing nothing but a background of stars. Wanda nodded. `Do nothing,' she said. `Say nothing until I have finished. And if you value your life, do not enter the pentagram, no matter what I do.'

Shrinkker nodded, went to his desk and sat down to watch and take notes.

Wanda gathered her robe around herself, walked to the console, and quickly tapped out commands on the keyboard. Then she stared hard at the screen and waited.

Shrinkker's original programme had come to him in one of those rare flashes of inspiration, wholly intuitive, and had seemed to him at the time one of those gifts from whatever Gods there were. It had been at odds with all his scientific training and experience, but he had tried it, and it had worked when coupled to the necessary electric power and equipment; the woman before him was living proof of that. But what he was now seeing was something else. He did not understand it. It shouldn't work. It defied logic. There were no spirits, no elemental forces, the supernatural did not exist in his book. And yet something did happen, and he was seeing it. Wanda Liszt, whose knowledge of computers was in the kindergarten class compared to his own, had somehow written a programme that achieved the unthinkable. She had harnessed one of those things that could not exist.

As he watched her, still and statuesque in the pentagram, he felt a cold finger trace down his spine, and the thought flickered through his mind that perhaps she had not written the programme; was she simply the instrument for something else, some dark force. The finger on his spine grew colder and he felt the hairs on his neck rise. He was a scientist, with all the courage sometimes needed when dealing with the unknown; but this was something else. He was fascinated, and determined to find the answers.

The star-studded screen saver image suddenly went opaque, dissolving into a swirling vortex of blue-green light. Shrinkker felt himself tense as Wanda stiffened, chin up and eyes narrowed. She bent forward and tapped a new command on the keyboard. The vortex swirled faster into a blur of light, and a dark core appeared, widening to fill the screen. Wanda smiled, tapped out another command, and waited. Moments later the screen brightened, steadied, and the blue monochrome changed to colour - a desert scene darkened by night, with only the brilliant illumination of stars to give substance to otherwise vague shapes. Shrinkker leant forward, hardly breathing, and totally conscious of the woman's warning.

Wanda Liszt peered intently at the image before her,

and then with a throaty sound of satisfaction, tapped another command. The image enlarged and zoomed in on a portion of the desert floor, allowing Shrinkker to see the outlines of sleeping bags beside a dying fire, and the square bulk of a LandRover. How it had happened he did not know, could not even guess; but he knew with certainty that some `eye' was projecting the scene through the computer to the screen. But what eye? The point of vision was at least fifty feet above the ground, and steady. One thing Shrinkker knew was that it was not a camera, and again he felt the hairs on his neck prickle.

The scene dissolved, to be replaced by the image of a large scale topographical map; and on it a point of light winked. At the bottom of the screen numbers appeared, and for the first time Wanda spoke, her voice husky and cold, devoid of emotion.

`Take these co-ordinates,' she ordered, and read the numbers to him as he scrabbled for his forgotten pencil and paper. Then she tapped a key on the board again and the map disappeared, to be replaced by the swirling vortex as Shrinkker wrote the last digit and looked up at her, swallowing nervously.

The vortex slowed and dissolved yet again into misty, rolling shapes like a dense fog bank. The shapes steadied and took on a form that was vaguely human; human in that there was a head, arms and a torso, but Shrinkker was mercifully too far to distinguish more. And then a voice spoke tinnily. Shrinkker jerked like a puppet with its strings pulled, stared at the screen in awful fascination, straining to hear words; but all he could distinguish was a sibilant jumble of noise in a language he did not recognize. Wanda listened intently, a half smile, wholly evil, on her face, and as the voice stopped, replied with just one word in the same hissing speech. Then the figure dissolved back to rolling fog, the vortex returned, slowed, and the screen went blank. Wanda Liszt tapped a key, the stars reappeared, and she relaxed, shoulders slumping. Slowly she gathered herself and turned.

`You saw?' she asked.

Shrinkker nodded. `What was ... ?' he began.

Wanda smiled. `Better you do not ask, my friend. Sufficient to say that I have learned what I wanted.'

She glanced once more at the screen and then stepped out of the pentagram, her hand outstretched. `The co-ordinates,' she demanded, and Shrinkker gave her the sheet of paper.

`How was the image obtained?' he asked. `There can have been no camera - not there.'

Wanda raised one beautiful curved eyebrow and gave a low laugh.

`Computers are tools, Professor, to be used. Who is to say that we mortals can be the only users?'

And with that she swept from the room leaving Shrinkker to stare after her, his mind a turmoil and none the wiser.

Wanda Liszt returned to the living chamber, poured herself a drink and lit a cigarette before dialling a single digit on the internal phone. She spoke briefly into it. `Send the pilot of the helicopter to me - now.'

CHAPTER ELEVEN

One second Gunn was asleep, enjoying comfort in a sleeping bag on stony ground that few men would have believed possible, and the next he was awake and shaking the Swede, his loaded and cocked M16 at the ready. He was listening as intently as a cat for the slight out-of-place sound that had penetrated his subconscious like a stiletto.

Tornquist surfaced like a hibernating bear. `What ...?'

`We've got company,' said Gunn. `You've got two minutes to be up in those rocks.' He pointed with the rifle to the small hill above them.

The Viking erupted from his bag with no further questions, grabbed his boots with one hand and caught the sub-machine gun Gunn had tossed him with the other. He hesitated, looked at the coffee pot sitting on the fire embers, then glanced at his two full hands and shrugged regretfully. The next second he was bounding into the rocks above the campsite like a great hairy troll.

In the meantime Gunn had crash-started the LandRover, spun its four wheels in the gravel, and skidded out of view behind a pile of rocks fifty yards away.

The thudding vibration of the helicopter rotor was clearly audible by the time he scrambled to safety near Tornquist.

`I should have listened to what my mother said,' he panted.

`Oh. What did she say?' asked Tornquist, a bit surprised to hear that Gunn even had a mother.

`I don't know,' Gunn replied, with a grin. `I never listened. But if I had it would probably have been to warn me about people like Wanda Liszt.'

`You think the chopper is to do with her?'

`I don't think,' Gunn replied. `I know.'

The noise in the helicopter cabin made conversation impossible, and the pilot pointed ahead to where a small group of stunted trees nestled beneath a craggy hill. He gave a thumbs up sign to his two companions. As they approached rapidly, skimming low like a giant dragon fly, they could just make out the shapes of two sleeping bags and camping gear through the first grey light of the approaching dawn. No-one noticed the missing LandRover.

The two men moved back into the body of the machine. The smaller of the two cocked a machine gun clipped on a swivel by the door, and cradled the stock against his shoulder, while the other pulled the pins from two L2A1 hand grenades. They balanced themselves and waited tensely as the helicopter swooped in for the attack.

The whiplash chatter of the machine gun shattered the still morning air, and the ground around the sleeping bags erupted into frenzied, boiling dust with the stream of bullets. Simultaneously, the hand grenades dropped and exploded, dead on target, in a flash of orange flame and a detonation that rocked the chopper as it stood on its rotor in a tight, skidding turn. Seconds later the process was repeated, and the machine hovered to a stop and lowered gently to the desert floor. The two men dropped out and scuttled forward in a low, crouching run.

Gunn put his hand on Tornquist's arm as he felt him tense, motioning him to wait. The men approached the shattered campsite carefully, each with a sub-machine gun at the ready, and then, detecting no signs of life, relaxed their guard.

At that instant Gunn raised the M16 and fired six carefully aimed and spaced shots, shouting as he did so for Tornquist to faze the helicopter.

With a muzzle velocity of 2,800 feet per second, nearly three times the speed of sound, the gunmen were thrown back by the hammer blows of the slugs without hearing a thing, and lay still. Gunn observed them without emotion for the space of a heartbeat, and then turned his attention to the helicopter and joined the Swede in added fire power to the already lethal hail from the Heckler and Koch.

The pilot, all too aware of the trap, was frantically trying to wind up the rotor to gain lift-off revolutions; but he was too late. Bullets smashed into the machinery, wrecking hydraulic lines and ripping gearing to shreds. The turbine started to screech as blades ripped off at high speed, black smoke began to pour from the engine cowlings, and then the fuel tank exploded and the whole thing disintegrated in a ball of orange flame.

As the echoes of the explosion died away and debris ceased to rain down, Torquil Tornquist stood up and looked at the weapon in his hands with an expression of mild surprise.

`That will teach them for waking us so early I think,' he said.

`Yes,' agreed Gunn. `I rather think it might.'

Tornquist was still looking at the sub-machine gun. `I did not know these things had so much power - to destroy a helicopter.'

`It was a civilian model,' Gunn replied. `No armour. And we were pretty damned close. And now, I think we'd better make tracks fairly smartly. When those jokers don't report to base, they just might come looking for us.'

`Which makes me wonder,' said Tornquist, as they made their way down to the camp. `Exactly how they found us in the first place.'

Gunn's face was grim as he replied. `It makes me wonder too. And I don't much like the thoughts I'm coming up with. Nobody, but nobody, knew we were here.'

Tornquist gave him a funny look. `Are you perhaps thinking that this business of Wanda Liszt may not be a story after all. You think maybe there is something about her that we do not understand.'

Gunn shrugged. `I don't know, but it sure as hell makes me wonder.'

`So, anyway, if they are going to come looking for us it might be a good idea if they found us, no?'

Gunn thought about that for a second, and then gave up. `I think you'd better explain yourself,' he said.

Tornquist pointed to a small cave entrance about a quarter of a mile away, not visible from the campsite, but quite apparent from their higher vantage point.

`And what's that?' Gunn asked.

`An old tomb.'

`How d'you know?'

`You forget I am an archaeologist.' Tornquist started for the cave with Gunn following. `Tombs have bones,' he said. `And with a little care we might be able to fool who ever comes looking. Fire is so very destructive, especially to human bodies. Maybe they will just count heads and won't look too closely.'

Gunn nodded. `It's a good idea. Certainly worth a try.'

Half an hour later, with the aid of some spare clothes and gasoline from the LandRover, they had managed a pretty fair deception. It wouldn't fool anyone who really looked, but then, who was going to. Burned bones looked much the same, no matter how old.

Tornquist dusted his hands on his pants and stood back to survey their handiwork. `Not bad,' he said. `And now we've also got a pretty fair idea which way to go. The chopper came from the east.'

`Once again you're right,' Gunn replied. `And it seems to confirm what you thought.' He started towards the LandRover. `We'd better get going.'

`But first we have breakfast, no?' the Swede shouted after him.

`If we can find any,' replied Gunn.

In the mouth of another desert tomb, not far from the one Gunn and Tornquist had been forced to desecrate, a shape, vaguely human and yet unlike anything of this earth, moved angrily as it saw the fireball from the exploding helicopter, and a long, sibilant sound of fury came from what might have been a mouth. For long moments it watched as the two men set about salvaging their camp and preparing breakfast, and then it moved away from the light of the new dawn till it was far back in the dark where no light had ever penetrated. It had a message to send to the woman creature with which it had so providentially joined.

The Thing was of limited intelligence, and like its kind needed a mind better than its own to operate outside the confines of the dimension in which it existed. In Wanda Liszt it had found that mind; one receptive to what it had to offer. With her it could have a being in Earth's time and space, and with it, she could aspire to power - at a price.

Though it did not understand computer programmes, or any of the mechanisms by which this dimension operated, it knew that to communicate with the woman it must put certain of its energy impulses into the box in the cavern. This it did.

Moments later a printer chattered, and a half dozen lines of incomprehensible wording appeared. Then the printer stopped, and the empty computer room fell silent once more.

Professor Edouard Shrinkker, coffee cup in hand, was the first to read the message when he unlocked the room some hours later. The words meant nothing to him, but he knew it was no code. He knew instinctively that it was to do with Wanda's scrying of the night before. With a slightly shaking hand he tore the sheet from the printer and left the room to find her.

Wanda Liszt read the message, and Shrinkker's nervousness increased as he saw her face turn white. She turned slowly to him, eyes narrowed and her mouth a thin scarlet line.

`You know what this is?' she hissed.

Shrinkker shook his head. `I can guess the origin, Lady, but not the content.'

`It's a message from...' She stopped in mid-sentence. `Never mind who from. And keep your guesses to yourself, understand.' Again she questioned him. `How much do you guess, Professor?'

`Enough, my Lady. I have eyes and ears - and imagination; but my tongue is silent.'

She nodded again, slowly. `See that it stays that way. And take care with your imagination. This thing is beyond your understanding - and control.'

Shrinkker swallowed nervously. `Am I permitted to know the content?' he asked.

Wanda slowly crumpled the paper into a tight ball, and then hurled it viciously into a corner. `It says that Maxim Gunn did not die in the ambush, nor did his companion.'

`This is a problem?'

Wanda raised an eyebrow, and then gave a harsh laugh. `Maxim Gunn is always a problem, Professor. Now please send the Baron to me.'

Shrinkker left the room immediately, and within minutes Baron von Gilderstein entered the room, hastily tying the belt on a silk dressing gown.

`What is it?' he asked, smoothing his elegant grey hair in a nervous gesture.

`Your plan failed,' Wanda said, bluntly.

The Baron sat down abruptly on the nearest chair.

`But it couldn't,' he stammered.

`It failed,' Wanda repeated, her voice rising.

The Baron salvaged just enough sense from his shock to refrain from repeating himself. Instead he asked how. He did not ask how she knew. Something told him that it would be better he did not know.

`Either they were waiting for the helicopter, or it crashed. Whichever it was does not matter, but I think the former.'

`But the attack was to be so sudden. They would have had no chance.'

Wanda slammed her hand on the drinks table, making the glasses jump. The Baron winced as if he had been struck. `Two men,' she screamed. `Asleep and totally unprepared, manage to wipe out three men and a heavily armed helicopter. Good God! I'm surrounded by imbeciles. A couple of boy scouts with slingshots could have done better.' She paused and lit a cigarette with trembling fingers. `And now Gunn knows where we are. Not exactly, maybe, but near enough. And knowing this he will stay on our trail - and nothing, but nothing, will make him let go except death. Gunn is a living example of the British Bulldog.'

The Baron prudently remained silent. He knew Wanda in her anger, and it was better to accept blame than argue. He was in a no-win situation and could only await her instructions. She ground out her cigarette angrily.

`You, Baron, may well fear our partners in this enterprise, and you are right to do so. But know this. In comparison to mine, their anger is nothing. Now, go to the site of the crash: find Maxim Gunn, and make sure that he does not discover this place. Do not fail me. You will not get another chance. And report to me the instant you return.'

The look on Wanda's face was enough. Her eyes glittered, and her face was a mask of white alabaster, the only colour the red slash of her lipstick. Without a word he left the chamber.

Wanda Liszt remained still for long moments after the Baron had left, her mind a seething cauldron of confused thoughts. Something within her refused to believe that Maxim Gunn had come into her life again. How could everything she hated most be personified behind his sardonic smile, which came to mock her even in her dreams. Each time she came within reach of triumph, he threw out his mocking challenge, and proceeded to wreck her carefully laid plans. And every time she had him beneath her hand, his destruction inevitable, the fates twitched the rug from under her feet and sent her sprawling, wrecked on the reef that was always waiting.

And now it seemed it was starting again; and she felt chilly foreboding reach out with clammy fingers.

She shook herself from the reverie, went to the sideboard, and though it was early in the day, splashed brandy into a glass and downed it at a single swallow. Then, calmer, she lit another cigarette and considered what had been achieved in the project so far, and what remained to be done. The minuses were starting to outweigh the pluses, and that was bad.

Project WORM was her brainchild, born of the realization that Professor Edouard Shrinkker had genuinely made a breakthrough, and was not just another crackpot peddling a pet theory. The acronym WORM appealed to her as appropriate when she thought of the mindless, struggling masses who fought for existence in the seething, overpopulated world outside her domain.

The World Organization for the Re-Education of Mankind was a magnificent conception, and worthy of even her father's genius. Many countries and political organizations would have jumped at her idea, but the problem had been to get the right partner; to play it her way and at her price. She felt she had made the right choice.

She had approached them through an ambassador whom she knew personally. He had been courteous, though not openly enthusiastic, and had passed her proposal and general terms to the appropriate quarter. Later she had been visited by a group of eminent psychologists under the leadership of a stony-faced individual referred to as the Colonel.

After her demonstration, which resulted in the death of a guard who had disobeyed orders, they had left, filled with a deep respect for the beautiful and dangerous woman. It was not long after that, that the Colonel had returned with direct orders. Equipment and funds quickly became available, and the caravansary had moved in great secrecy to the present site. She felt it appropriate that the birth of the New Order should occur in the tomb of the once-great king.

Shrinkker's discovery was going to be truly earth-shaking, and she was determined that nothing would stop her. Her partners had supplied the money and equipment, but she had no intention of letting them take control. That was to be hers alone; they were to be used.

She shivered suddenly, as if someone had walked over her grave, and little ghostly fingers of doubt tickled the back of her mind. She knew the cause, immediately and instinctively. Maxim Gunn. She dropped her cigarette on the white rug, stamped on it, and swept out of the chamber, closing the door with a bang.

It was many hours later that a very weary and dusty Baron von Gilderstein finally returned to the caverns. His miserable journey by jeep through the heat of the arid, stony country had paid off though, and he was able to report to his mistress that, despite the loss of the helicopter and three men, he could also confirm the presence of two other charred corpses. Maxim Gunn and Torquil Tornquist the Swede, were also dead. The helicopter might have crashed, or been shot down, but in the process the end result had been satisfactory. The burning wreckage must have completed the job.

As Gunn had hoped, the Baron had not examined the evidence too closely.

Wanda was reluctant to accept the news, instinctively wary, and doubtful even in the face of the Baron's report. The Dark Force, her alter ego from the computer, had told her differently. Could it be wrong? It seemed too coincidental, too easy an answer. But she also knew Maxim Gunn. Had he worked some trick to fool her, even now? Still, the evidence was there though she was reluctant to accept it.

Wanda stood up, signalling that the meeting was at an end. `Baron. I want you to personally ensure that all security arrangements are tightened and rechecked. The entire success of the operation hinges on the next phase in Washington and Paris - I have made other plans for the British Prime Minister. Nothing can be allowed to interfere.'

`But, my Lady, with Gunn out of the way ...'

`Nothing,' she snapped, and swept out.

CHAPTER TWELVE

Maxim Gunn and Torquil Tornquist breakfasted scratchily from a couple of tins and lukewarm coffee, and got underway without further trouble. The attack had made no difference to their general plan, apart from confirming the direction they were aiming for.

Gunn drove, part of his attention on the bumping track, and part on what Tornquist was saying. The big Swede was delivering a monologue, more in the manner of thinking aloud than caring if he got answers. He was dredging his vast storehouse of archaeological and mythological knowledge of the area in an effort to pinpoint the location of the great tomb with some kind of accuracy. So far, he was having little success, and Gunn was beginning to wonder what kind of miracle would be needed if he was going to pull this thing off in time. And that was the unknown factor: timing. What the hell was Wanda's timing? The early morning attack told him that he still had some to spare, or else why bother. And how much would her plans have been either put back, or brought forward by the frustration of the Prime Minister's cancellation? No way of telling. All he could do was plug on and pray the extraordinary man muttering to himself in the passenger seat would come up with the necessary miracle.

The other unsettling thought was the ease with which they had been found at the camp-site. Gunn was more concerned about that than he had cared to admit. They had seen no-one the previous day, and he was morally certain no-one had seen them. Hesitantly, he reached inside his shirt and touched Termaxian's amulet.

Miles behind them, in the other desert tomb, the Thing saw the Baron and, reading his thoughts, chuckled. There was no hurry to communicate with the woman creature again, and it would not move from the tomb until darkness came.

The morning wore on and the heat intensified; but apart from a brief stop for coffee, and to fill the tank from their spare jerry cans, they had pressed on without wasting time. Gunn's basic idea was to quarter the area the helicopter was most likely to have come from, he knew it couldn't have come all that far as it was a type of fairly limited range, and the fireball from the exploding tanks had indicated a pretty full load of fuel. He had been more than a little interested to note that it was a Russian machine, a Mil Mi2, code name Hoplite. By itself that meant nothing, but Gunn knew large sales had been made in the time of the Old Guard. The knowledge served to confirm Vileman's worst fears that Wanda had gone into an unholy alliance. He chuckled and thought that it was always the other side who were the bad guys; and would the alliance have been any better if Wanda had gone to his own government for support. Probably not. Power was power, in any language.

A crashing thud as the front wheels hit a pothole brought him back to the job in hand, and he swore; then noticed his companion was behaving in a peculiar way, muttering excitedly and continually twisting and turning in all directions as if he was trying to spot something he knew ought to be there. He was about to speak when the Swede said sharply. `We must move carefully, Maxim. Something tells me we are getting near.'

`I sort of noticed that,' Gunn replied, with a smile. `Cats on hot bricks would be positively restful compared to you.' But he took the warning seriously. The man had a hunch, and Gunn trusted hunches. His own sixth sense was highly developed.

The sun was approaching its highest point when they pulled to a stop in the shade of a couple of stunted thorn trees near the base of a cliff. What shade there was, was welcome, and the two men got out to ease cramped muscles and have a lunch break. As they sipped hot black coffee and munched biscuits and tinned meat, Tornquist paced restlessly, still muttering to himself in a personal argument, while Gunn relaxed and minutely scanned the surrounding hills through powerful binoculars.

Suddenly his attention was caught by a small plateau area beneath the beetling height of a dark cliff, and he got up quickly and went to the LandRover. Moments later he was back with the photos Vileman had given him in London, and compared them to the cliff in front. There was no doubt about it. The time of day was different as indicated by the shadows, and there was no sign of Bill Henderson's body, but it was undoubtedly the same place. He turned to Tornquist and called urgently, his voice tight with satisfaction.

`Eureka. It looks like we're on the right track, my friend. Take a look at these.' He passed the photos to Tornquist who came lumbering over. The big man took them and made the same minute comparison, then smiled back. `So. We have made it, no?'

Gunn shook his head. `No. Now we know we're on the right track. This is the place Henderson died; but is it the site of Wanda's headquarters?'

Tornquist's enthusiasm was not dampened. `Of course it is. She made a mistake in sending those photos. A case of hubris, false pride. You will see.' He slapped Gunn's shoulder hard, making him flinch. `Come. We must start.'

Gunn held up a restraining hand. `No. We're pretty much too close for comfort. You can be certain there are guards around. Wanda is not stupid. And what about the other thing?'

Tornquist's mouth twitched inside his beard, and he raised a shaggy eyebrow. `So. You think something other than little men with rifles may watch as well?'

Gunn sighed, and for one of the few times in his life felt confused and at a loss for positive words. `Damned if I know.' And looking hard at Tornquist, asked. `Didn't you wonder, just a little bit, how that helicopter found us so easily? I know we weren't followed.'

Tornquist frowned and scratched his head. `So. If that is the case, she probably knows we are here anyway. We must confront her.'

Gunn gestured at the cliff. `Fine. If this is the place we still have to locate an entrance. What do you suggest? That we stand up and shout an invitation? If she's half the person she used to be - and I think she's more than she used to be - we'll get blown out of the water, so to speak. I've said it once, and I'll reinforce it. Wanda Liszt is damned dangerous. He got up and slipped the photos back in the envelope. `What we do now is lie low and wait for dark - it's a lot too hot to go leaping around anyway. I'll get the LandRover out of sight in the shadows and we'll wait it out.'

The rest of the long, hot afternoon was spent in the illusion of cool in the gloom beneath the cliff. Tornquist was edgy, though not through fear of what might happen; fear was something quite alien to his nature. Rather he was anxious about what he hoped he might discover, and the thought of presenting the discovery of the Tomb of Gilgamesh to the world had all but driven thoughts of the true purpose of the exercise from his mind. As Gunn had said earlier, such a find would put him in the ranks of Carter and Schliemann, the finders of Tutankhamen and Troy, only more so. It would be like finding Atlantis; a legend brought to life. But Gunn's quiet reminder had made him think. It also made him very determined that whatever secrets might be there would be his, and he wasn't going to let this woman, Wanda Liszt, get in his way.

Gunn, for his part, fully aware of the dangers, had spent his time resting and checking their weapons. Like any good soldier he knew the value of rest and preparation. He made no attempt to draw the Swede back into the dark world inhabited by evil creatures like Wanda Liszt, for he had done his part and done it nobly, though there was still more to come. Without him, Gunn would still have been casting around in Ankara, looking for a lead. That he would have eventually found what he was looking for he did not doubt, but it might have been too late. Wanda's plan to gain control of the British Prime Minister had shown that her operation was close to getting underway, and whatever her timing, without Tornquist he could never have got this close so fast. As the shadows deepened and stretched further to the east, he turned on his side, propped himself on one elbow, and said. `It's going to be dark soon. What we'll do is reconnoitre around and on top of the cliff. You go along the base, and I'll get on top as I'm probably the better climber. We'll go a set distance each way - say an hour, and look for any signs of human activity. For instance, they must have parked that helicopter somewhere, so there may be oil spills, foot marks, something to give that away, and they may have left tire tracks to and from the entrance. I may spot them from the top, but you should have a better chance at ground level. Look hard, Torquil, and use that famous clue finding brain. We'll meet back here at midnight. Oh, and there'll be a moon tonight, so be careful and use cover. Keep out of sight. As I said, there'll be guards, and our best hope is surprise.'

Tornquist had come back to the present and the job in hand, and listened intently to what Gunn said. He had the sense to realize he was dealing with things outside his experience. Nevertheless he grinned. `And if she has already seen us in her crystal ball, or whatever?'

`We'll cross that bridge, if it happens,' Gunn replied, a

little uncomfortably.

`What if one of us gets caught?'

`The other waits till dawn and then hightails it back to Adana. Memorize this phone number.' And he gave it to the Swede. `It's my contact in London. Put them in the picture.'

`How will they know who I am?'

`They already know,' Gunn replied. `But you're assuming it's me that's going to get caught. It might be you. And better still, neither of us.'

`At least that way I would get inside.'

`Then the trick would be to get out again,' said Gunn, dryly.

They had a quick meal, gathered their weapons, and, as night finally fell, Gunn set out to make his way to the cliff top. Tornquist waited half an hour as agreed to give Gunn time, and then he too left, like a Viking marauder scouting an enemy shore.

The moon was rising as Gunn reached the top of the cliff. It had been easier than he imagined, but longer, as he had had to make one wide detour around a deep ravine, and as a result he was later than planned. By the time he was able to reconnoitre the dark depths below the face and pinpoint Tornquist, the Swede was well ahead.

Lying on the edge he looked down at the spot where Bill Henderson had met his end, and searched for marks, any indication that there might have been a struggle. But there was nothing, which was curious in itself as Bill was not a man to have gone easily. He didn't pursue the matter, but instead concentrated on searching the moonlit ground far below for some sign of a path or vehicle tracks.

He could just make out Tornquist's shadowy bulk moving ahead, a pretty obvious target to Gunn's trained eye, and could see he was making for the small plateau they had noticed earlier, and which they had decided might be a helicopter pad. He slid back out of sight and moved forward quickly to catch up with Tornquist.

By the time he saw the danger it was to late. Too late to even shout a warning, though to have done so would have given himself away. As Tornquist moved from shadow and began to cross the small open plateau, Gunn saw two figures emerge from behind a large boulder, and even at the distance he was he could clearly distinguish the distinctive shapes of the Kalashnikov AK-47 assault rifles they carried. There was nothing to do except watch in mute agony as they advanced on the Swede. Moments later Tornquist sensed their presence and whirled, and he too realized there was nothing he could do that would not have been suicidal; and in response to some unheard command Gunn watched helplessly as he let the M16 drop, and slowly raised his hands.

Gunn had half expected to hear the staccato hammer of gunfire, but instead, the two men, one on each side and at a safe distance, marched their prisoner down an ill-defined track towards the sheer cliff face. He watched in anticipation.

The fact that Tornquist had so easily been caught was bad, very bad, and spoke either of an efficient guard system, or ... and he shook the thought from his mind. But there was a chance that the hidden entrance would be revealed, and that was what he needed to both get himself in, and Tornquist out. Gunn thought that whatever entrance there was would have to be very well concealed to have remained undiscovered for so many long centuries.

At the base of the cliff the prisoner and escort stopped, and one of the men took something from his pocket. It looked like a small walkie-talkie. He appeared to speak briefly into it.

Nothing happened for a couple of minutes, and then,

silently, a dark crack appeared in the rock face, and a huge slab moved slowly to one side revealing an opening big enough to have driven a truck through. The trio went inside and vanished, and then the slab returned ponderously back into place, leaving a blank and featureless wall of rock.

Gunn found he had been holding his breath throughout the entire episode, and released it explosively.

`Well, I'll be damned,' he murmured. `Talk about "Open Sesame" '.

He waited long moments, thinking furiously, and knowing that despite seeing what he had he would never get in that way, as there would be some code word to whoever operated the opening mechanism inside.

And then he thought of Bill Henderson. He'd got in, and probably not through the front door either. Gunn racked his brains for an answer, and then got the glimmer of an idea. People in caves breathed air, just like anyone else, and he'd been down enough mines and other underground systems to know they all had ventilation shafts or airways. This place had to be the same. Airway in and airway out. The old tomb makers might not have bothered, but Wanda would. All he had to do was find them, and in the dark of an unfamiliar cliff top that was going to be next to impossible. He decided to find shelter from the night wind and start his search at first light. It looked like being a miserable night, as not only was the wind rising, but there was the flicker of lightning on the horizon and he could smell a suggestion of rain in the air. On balance however, he thought he'd rather be cold and wet and on the outside, than warm and Wanda's prisoner.

He finally settled on a small, sandy depression between two boulders and composed himself to wait out the hours till dawn and do some hard thinking. Not that there was really all that much to think about he realized; it was getting to be a do or die situation. The points he came up with were as follows:

One: He had to get into the cavern undetected - probably impossible as Wanda seemed to have the help of the ... He stopped that line of thought. Anyway, she'd know he was there. And getting down an air shaft - how narrow, he wondered - should be easy for anyone with fantastic rock climbing ability and suicidal tendencies.

Two: He had to find the vital equipment, presumably after having put Wanda and her crew out of action, and wreck it beyond hope. Or, better still, lift it and get it back to London. Again, easy for anyone with a Doctorate in Computer Science who could sort out what was probably down there, and had a squad of Commandos at his heels. On the whole Gunn fancied a nice heavy crowbar.

Three: Get Tornquist out with his momentous news of the tomb's discovery. He was under no illusion that this was going to be high on the Swede's list of priorities.

Four: Get rid of Wanda Liszt, the Baron and Professor Shrinkker - finally.

All of which should add up to a nice morning's work which he should be able to knock off sometime between breakfast and lunch.

He gave a mental shrug and settled himself against a boulder and closed his eyes just as the first fat drops of rain splashed coldly down, and thunder crashed above him like a naval barrage.

CHAPTER THIRTEEN

While Maxim Gunn slept fitfully on the wet, windy cliff top, Torquil Tornquist was, although admittedly warmer, certainly no more comfortable.

He had been marched through the cavern entrance by his two guards, and only the presence of the Kalashnikovs had prevented him from picking the pair of them up and turning them into human pretzels. He didn't take kindly to being prodded and pushed.

A very brief interview with Wanda Liszt had ended with his being thrown into a bare chamber for the rest of the night, under lock and key, with a double guard on the door who were under no illusion as to their fate should he be allowed to as much as blink.

Wanda's rage had been spectacular, and the Baron had been left in no doubt as to his ability to organize security, and had learned some interesting, but highly improbable things about the habits of his ancestors. Auntie de Lorian, who until then had been keeping well in the background, had undeservedly caught the backlash, and been told she was without doubt a candidate for a home for incurable geriatrics, and would be saving everyone a lot of trouble if she jumped off the nearest cliff. The guards had been praised, much to their surprise, and were now giving good imitations of a pair of Dobermann Pinschers.

Throughout the tirade, Tornquist had sat open-mouthed with admiration, and was even then wondering whether he had fallen in love. Such spirit, such command. Well, you never knew, he thought as he sat in his lonely cell; the woman had the most gigantic ego that maybe he could flatter her enough to get a stay of execution and give Gunn time to come galloping to the rescue like the cavalry.

Whatever the final outcome - and he had little doubt that she would finally dispose of him - if she thought he was securely out of action for the time being, he might get a chance to find out where the nerve centre was, and do a bit of wrecking on his own account. He had no intention of going to Valhalla without a fight. And with those thoughts whirling around in his head, he drifted into peaceful slumber and dreamed of Wanda's dark beauty.

Some hours later, Gunn woke to a bright, cold dawn, washed clean by the night's storm, and stretched cold-stiffened limbs. His soul craved for a cup of hot coffee and a hot shower. He shrugged; it was going to be one of those days.

Dawn brought nothing in the way of an indication as to where the air vents might be, but then he knew they would no doubt be well concealed, and on the windward side at that, to catch the prevailing breeze. With all the care of a Sioux scout, he made his way round the cliffs until he was on the far side of the ravine, with a good view of the huge cliff face in which the mysterious door had appeared. And there he waited.

Now, in the poor shade of a small bush, he eased cramped muscles and removed a minute pebble from under his hip-bone. The noon sun, having burnt away the morning chill, was intense, and his eyes ached with the strain of looking. His faded khaki shirt and trousers, tucked into scuffed leather boots, blended perfectly with the dun-coloured rocks of his surroundings. He rubbed tired eyes, and once again lifted the powerful binoculars to rake the jumbled scree on the far side of the ravine.

Somewhere over there had to be the airways - well camouflaged, but most certainly there.

By then his whole being ached for a cold drink. He decided to give it another hour, and then get back to Adana for some additional equipment - such as ropes -

some sleep, and a bit of thinking in comfort. He knew if he didn't find the air vents in the next short while, he would only be knocking himself out pointlessly by staying where he was, and incidentally increase his chances of being found. Wanda had Tornquist, and she would know that he, Gunn, wouldn't be far away. Better she should waste her energies, and those of her men, in trying to find him, while he built up his reserves for an all out effort. He would return in the early hours of the next morning, and with luck, the warmer air from the complex buried in the cliff would cause a slight fog as it came out. His only alternative was to spend hours crawling the cliff top, avoiding search parties, in the hope of stumbling over what he wanted.

Gunn wasn't worried about Tornquist for the time being, as he felt certain Wanda would try to get all the information out of him she could, plus, of course, using him as a lure. Tornquist might have a bit of a rough time of things, but nothing he couldn't handle; and besides, he had known what he was getting into.

Finally he moved, counted slowly to one hundred, and then eased back cautiously from the ravine edge and stood up. It would take the better part of an hour to get back to the LandRover, and then, by taking the quick route, there was another three hour drive over poorish roads till he reached the hotel.

He stuffed the binoculars back in their case, dusted off his trousers, and started off briskly down the slope, eyes peeled for any sign of movement that would betray a search party.

As he jogged over the stony ground, making practiced use of the land to stay as much in cover as possible, he thought back over the chain of events that had brought him to that arid and ancient part of the world.

Wanda Liszt was on the loose again, returned from the

dead apparently, and about to raise more devils - he smiled grimly at the choice of words - than the history of the world had ever known; and she had to be stopped. The knowledge that he was the only person who could do it brought little comfort. He was out-numbered, and out-gunned - not in itself an unusual state of affairs; but this time she had thrown in her lot with one of the world's great powers, and her plan was the total slavery of mankind. The word, power, jerked at his conscious yet again. It had different connotations this time, and once again he slid his hand into his shirt-front, and wondered at the extra-ordinary comfort he got from the little amulet dangling against his skin. Time. Time. What time did he have?

He quickened his pace until it would have taken a superbly trained cross-country athlete to match his easy stride. But then he was driven by a prize greater than mere records and adulation. And continually the name drummed through his mind like the beat of a railway carriage over tracks at high speed. Wanda Liszt ... Wanda Liszt ... Wanda Liszt.

Over two thousand miles away, in London, Vileman sat at his desk and drummed impatient fingers on the leather top. Then he leant forward, pressed a button on the intercom, and snarled.

`Chief of Staff?'

`It had better be,' came the reply. `Or there's someone in my office who shouldn't be.'

Vileman sighed. `Spare me the jokes, Boone, and get up here.'

`Your wish is my command, Oh Master.'

`Move it, will you,' Vileman snapped, and punched the off button. Then he leant back and gave vent to another massive sigh, wondering why it was he was afflicted by insubordination at all levels. One of these days, he thought, I'll get rid of Boone. But he knew he wouldn't. His

Yorkshire Chief of Staff was a rare jewel, with an ability to cut to the root of any problem, and a total disrespect for authority and the ways of the Establishment that enabled him to short cut accepted channels without a qualm. In anyone else such behaviour would have spelt disaster from a career point of view; but the fact was that Boone just didn't care about such things, so he got away with it. And thinking about insubordination brought his thoughts back to Maxim Gunn. A year ago Gunn had announced his resignation, and quit. At first Vileman had been thrilled, as he'd finally got rid of the one man who really put his back up, and who he could never get the better of. But since then, he had the grace to realize that the agent was badly missed, and strangely, it had been easy to go to him for help, however unofficial.

And that was what he was worrying about when there was a knock on the door and Indigo Boone sauntered in, his pipe giving a fair imitation of a coal-fired blast furnace. Boone crossed the room and slumped into a chair, hands stuffed into his pockets. Vileman coughed exaggeratedly and waved his hands to clear the air.

`For God's sake, Chief,' he coughed. `There's more than enough damned pollution in the world without you adding to it. Anyway, what kept you?'

Boone looked at him with a mixture of pity and contempt. Boone was an avid cricket enthusiast, and totally unable to understand anyone who felt otherwise. He knocked his pipe into the ashtray.

`The M.C.C. have got the Aussies on the run. We're making mincemeat of their bowlers. I had to wait till the end of the over.'

Vileman stiffened, and his face coloured. `The whole damned world's about to go down the drain if Gunn can't pull this thing off in time, and all you can do is listen to a stupid cricket match? It's a miserably silly game not fit for two-year-olds, let alone grown men.'

`This match will decide the Ashes,' Boone replied, with a look that Medusa could have learned a thing or two from. `And as for Gunn; what can we do to help by worrying?'

`The Ashes,' Vileman snapped, referring to the annual matches between Britain and Australia. `The whole world's going to be ashes before we know it, and you ...'

`What did you want?' interrupted Boone.

`What did I ...? WHERE'S GUNN?'

`Turkey.' Boone answered, evenly.

`God help us. I know that. But where? And what's he up to there? Playing cricket for all I know.'

`They don't play cricket in Turkey,' said Boone, crushingly.

Vileman lowered his head onto his hands and groaned in despair. Then he straightened briskly. The game was over; it was time to get down to business. He felt better.

`O.K. Chief of Staff. Just what do we know?'

Boone took out his pipe and refilled it, and then, in between puffs as he lit it, said. `Not much. In fact nothing since his call from Adana giving us the lovely news about the Prime Minister.'

Vileman shuddered at the thought; about what might have been if Gunn had not got through. The P.M. had been somewhat acid when he'd put him in the picture, just as he was about to get into his car to go to the performance. But he had obeyed him, and immediately cancelled. He was like that, and took advice from those he put in positions such as Vileman held - though they were few.

Boone continued. `We know he's with this Tornquist character, and they're going to do a search in the Taurus mountains.'

`A bloody big area to search,' mused Vileman.

`Happen Gunn and this fellow have narrowed it down a bit, or they'll be there till they grow long beards.'

`Why would Gunn have teamed up with a fella like

that?' asked Vileman. `It's not like him to use help. He's always been a loner.'

Boone shook his head. `I don't know about that. He uses who he needs. What about Siriani, among others?'

`But why an archaeologist. He's not looking for ruins.'

`Maybe he is,' Boone replied, and seeing Vileman's puzzlement, expanded. `I've an idea this operation of Wanda's has got to be big, and by that I mean it's going to take up room, and that means hiding it. The whole area down there is littered with ancient remains - caves and ruins. Maybe this Tornquist has given Gunn an idea, and he thinks he can help him find it.'

Vileman sighed with exasperation. `Why does he always have to play it so close. He knows what it does to me.'

Boone grinned and puffed explosively on his pipe. `Probably why he always did it. But any road, have you ever known him to be wrong? Can't say I have. And you can bet he won't be wasting time on wild goose chases. He knows the importance of speed in this thing.'

Vileman slumped. `No. I've never known him wrong, and that's what I used to hate about him most. You know, just once I'd like to see him fall on his face. But I know I never will.' And he held up his hand before Boone could protest. `No, Chief of Staff, I didn't mean that. It's just the spiteful old man in me.'

`I know,' Boone replied. `And we won't know anything till he tells us.'

`Then we'll have to bite the bullet and wait. And in the meantime keep the P.M. off our backs. If I were a praying man, which I'm not, I'd be on my knees right now. We've never had a worse one than this.'

`Except when Australia last won the Ashes,' replied Boone, with a smile. And with that he got up and left, leaving Vileman wishing he had the Yorkshireman's laid back attitude. He had deliberately refrained from raising his other fears about Gunn's mission; his fears that this time they might have bitten off something that was bigger than mortal man could handle. What if, he thought, there really was something to the business of Wanda and...?

Very deliberately and firmly he put such thoughts aside. There was enough to worry about without conjuring phantoms. He gazed for a long moment at the door his Chief of Staff had softly closed on his way out, and then took a file from his in-tray and switched his mind to yet another problem.

CHAPTER FOURTEEN

Dusk was settling and throwing purple shadows, and the first of the evening folk were emerging when Gunn awoke, refreshed, at precisely the time he had planned. His built in mental timer made an alarm clock unnecessary. He showered, changed, had a quick meal, and five minutes after paying his bill, drove off back in the direction of the mountains.

Five miles north of the town he pulled in at an orange grove, and was met by two villainous looking men, who passed over the items he had arranged through Rostov's contact man, Kemel.

A few eyebrows might have been raised among the authorities if they had known what those items were, and a certain amount of alarm might have been felt had they known that such things were so readily available. But Gunn, like most people in his world, knew that anything could be had if you had the right contacts, and the price.

He lifted his hand in salute to the men, and left, the LandRover's headlights cutting into the velvety warm darkness ahead. He had a sense of direction like a homing pigeon, and the thought that he might lose his way after only one short visit to the cliff site did not even enter his head. He had plenty of time to get into position before dawn, though he was concerned that the time for getting Tornquist out, and for putting a massive spoke in Wanda's wheel, was probably running out fast. He knew that he would either find what he was looking for next morning at sunrise, or, well, he might just have to go and get himself caught too. At least that way he'd be sure of getting inside whatever it was.

In the desert tomb, the Thing stirred, smelling the darkness that was its familiar world. It knew the time had come to leave the cave and make its way to where the woman creature was. It also knew that all was not right with her, and that its presence was needed. As it moved to the cave mouth and saw, without curiosity or wonder, the million bright pin lights of the stars, it sensed that the woman was once again trying to reach it, and it lifted its obscene travesty of a face to home on the direction of the insistent call.

Being of a different dimension, and obeying physical laws unknown to humans, it lifted itself into the night air and swiftly moved in the direction of the great tomb of Gilgamesh.

In the depths of the tomb, Wanda's first terrible anger had diminished, but was still enough in evidence to ensure she was given a wide berth by all except Professor Shrinkker, and she had spent the entire day locked with him in the computer chamber, checking and re-checking her plans; making doubly sure that all the final details were taken care of.

The Baron had been unusually conscientious, and after a day of thoroughly irritating all the guards, was now awaiting her arrival in the main room of the living quarters, prepared to give her his report on the revised and tightened security arrangements. Auntie de Lorian was also in the room, having memorized the dossiers of each person she was to contact and bug. She was knitting an ill-defined article with patent lack of concentration, as she jumped at every sharp sound and snapped at the Baron when he so much as coughed.

The angry rapping of high heels in the corridor outside the chamber made them both stiffen and look at each other anxiously.

The doors banged open and Wanda swept in on the

nervous hush inside. `Well?' she demanded. `I trust you have both carried out your orders.'

They both swallowed nervously, and nodded, and the Baron sprang to his feet to get her a drink and a cigarette. She accepted both without thanking him, and flung herself onto the settee.

`As even your minuscule brains will have realized,' she began, sarcasm dripping from her words, `the reason I have not disposed of that mountainous oaf, Tornquist, is in order to extract information from him. Twenty-four hours of solitary confinement will have begun to prey on his nerves. He will be wondering. He will be getting anxious. So, after dinner, we shall pay him a visit.' She paused, dramatically. `If the information I want is not forthcoming, very quickly, I shall extract it by other means, and he will follow the fate of the late Henderson.'

`So quickly?' asked de Lorian.

Wanda's reply was withering. `Later, it would have no value. Surely even you see that. Gunn will already have arrived.'

`What about Gunn?' the Baron asked.

`Indeed,' Wanda replied, silkily. `You may well ask. Despite your unbelievable ineptitude, the cards will fall our way, my way. He will have reasoned that this is what I shall do, and will no doubt make an all out effort to rescue this Tornquist. Gunn is loyal to his companions, you see.' The Baron and de Lorian thought, but refrained from saying, that in that he differed greatly from Wanda Liszt. She continued. `We shall be ready for him, and then I shall carry out what you, Baron, appear to be incapable of. I shall execute him.'

The Baron once again refrained from the obvious remarks that her attempts on Gunn's life, in Ankara, had also been singularly unsuccessful. There was a time when he might have pointed this out to her, but this was a new Wanda, and he was afraid. The memory of the manner of Bill Henderson's death, and the control she could exert over his mind, among others, was enough to stop him reminding her of anything but her successes.

`But Gunn cannot get into the tomb, my Lady,' said Auntie de Lorian.

Wanda closed her eyes as if tired, and said with utmost clarity. `Don't use the word cannot with regard to Maxim Gunn. He will get in, despite your efforts, Baron. Though how, I do not know.' She glanced sharply at her unhappy lieutenant. `All entrances are secured and guarded. You have posted lookouts above?'

`All is taken care of, my Lady,' the Baron assured her, eagerly.

`See that it is. Gunn will get in, however, and I want him to, and then we shall seal the place tighter than Fort Knox. Not so much as a beetle will get out unnoticed.' Then she smiled evilly. `The Professor assures me the Treasure Room mechanisms are still in a remarkable state of preservation. Everything still works perfectly it seems. Gunn will be allowed to demonstrate just how the ancients guarded their valuables.'

She held her glass out to the Baron. `Another drink if you please. I feel this time I shall finally be rid of Maxim Gunn. The Treasure Room was a lucky find.'

`Not so lucky for the man who found it,' Auntie murmured.

`It taught him not to be inquisitive,' came the sharp reply.

Meanwhile, locked away in his lonely prison, Torquil Tornquist was suffering none of the mental anguish Wanda had so fondly imagined. In his brief acquaintance with Gunn, he had formed an inexplicable faith in the ex-agent's abilities; a faith which Gunn would have found touching, if rather misguided, and anyway, he was not a man to worry when there was nothing he could do. He was, however, suffering from a totally different kind of anguish, hunger. His was a large frame, which needed vast quantities of solid sustenance at regular intervals, as Gunn had observed, and now, after nearly twenty-four hours of enforced fast, his stomach was beginning to inform him it thought his throat had been cut; and this was making him edgy. And an edgy Tornquist was about as safe to handle as a case of old and sweaty dynamite.

The guard who unlocked and opened the cell door to take him to Wanda Liszt, never really knew what hit him. The door flew back the second the catch was released, and took him squarely in the face with the force of a steam locomotive piston at speed, and the luckless man was catapulted backwards like a shell from a naval gun. In his unconscious flight, he flattened the Baron, caught the Professor a glancing blow which made his teeth rattle, and finally finished up with a jarring smack against the far wall, dislodging a lump of rock which had resisted gravity for several thousand years.

Tornquist emerged and stood for a split second, surveying the startled faces of Wanda Liszt and Auntie de Lorian through the dust of his eruption. Then the door creaked and clattered to the floor as its hinges gave way and the thick oak panels splintered. With a roar he took off like a charging rhino down the passage, a variety of half-formed thoughts flashing through his mind, among which food loomed with exaggerated importance.

Wanda's shriek of alarm alerted a number of other guards in the vicinity, and in a short time Tornquist was cornered in the main living-room.

The fight which preceded his ultimate capture took considerably longer, and in the process caused the total destruction of a desk, three chairs and a standard lamp; together with severe damage to five of the guards.

He was finally subdued when Wanda, who had prudently stayed out of the thick of the fight, crept round behind him as he was crushing the life from another guard in a gigantic bear hug, and forcefully applied a desk leg to the back of his skull. He went down like a felled tree, and in the process wrecked her settee.

The rising moon was turning the landscape into something an astronaut might have stepped onto, when Maxim Gunn finally returned to the cliff site at about the same time that Tornquist was showing off his strength in the living quarters. He lit a small butane stove in the lee of the LandRover, made coffee and drank some, and poured the rest into a large thermos flask. It looked like being another long, cold night, and he saw no percentage in being more miserable than he had to. Then he gathered his equipment and began the long climb back up the cliff.

An hour later he was nearing his last night's position, and began to be more than usually careful. Wanda would certainly know he was around, and there would inevitably be patrols or guards, and it was very necessary that he saw them before they saw him.

He wondered about Tornquist, and was smiling to himself as he eased forward from the cover of a crop of boulders, thinking she might have bitten off more than she could comfortably chew, when a movement at the corner of his eye made him freeze, and curse himself for allowing his attention to wander.

The guard - for that's who it was - moved out of the protective shelter of a large rock, and Gunn blessed that age old enemy of all night guards - boredom. How often had he drummed into the skulls of trainees he'd been called upon to lecture, that being on watch meant exactly that. Watching was done with the eyes; and the fact that you were cold, wet, scared or just plain bored, didn't matter. The object was to see and not be seen. The night was on your side, and unless the other fellow had eyes like a cat, if you kept still, his chances of seeing you first were nearly nil.

The man lit a cigarette, and Gunn made a low, throaty sound of contempt. Night vision gone, and his presence made obvious, all for the sake of a few lungs full of smoke. The brief flare of the match showed a vicious, rat-like face, with a long, thin nose and lank fair hair. Gunn didn't think his passing would be mourned by many, and stayed in his cover, thinking. With the man's night vision temporarily destroyed, Gunn could probably have walked right up to him, but his movements over the next couple of minutes would have earned the respect of most ghosts; and the effect of his voice saying, almost conversationally, in the man's ear that smoking could be a health hazard, was most gratifying. The guard broke all known records for the standing high jump, and then collapsed in a heap as Gunn chopped him expertly behind the ear.

Gunn looked down at the crumpled body at his feet, and murmured grimly. `See, what did I tell you?'

He moved quickly away after rolling the body into a crack between two rocks. There would probably be others in the area, and they might well have a contact schedule; in which case he wanted to pinpoint as many as possible - and deal with them.

But there were no further incidents, and he was forced to reason that the man had been the only one on the cliff top; and that led him to reason further that Wanda must feel totally secure from that direction as far as a forced entry was concerned. It looked as if he was going to have to prove her wrong.

Gunn took up a position from where he could see the great sliding door. No-one came out or went in for the rest of the night. He was reasonably sure that Wanda Liszt was still inside, and that the guard, who had probably been a junior and told to stay put till relieved, had not been missed. There would no doubt be a change after dawn, and by then he knew he would have to be inside anyway.

He firmly put aside all thoughts of his own comfort, and settled down to obey his own teachings, and watch. One thing he was sure of though, was that the great tomb would be under maximum security, like a prison for psychotics and other dangerous criminals; and that as in all such places, maximum security bred complacency. Somewhere there would be an overlooked way in, or one so impossible as to be disregarded, such as the air shaft he was hoping to find.

CHAPTER FIFTEEN

As the first grey shades began to lighten the eastern sky, Maxim Gunn stretched and worked his muscles to restore circulation. He picked up the flask, poured the last dregs of lukewarm coffee into the cup, and swallowed with a grimace.

Nothing had moved during the night, not so much as a small animal, and he knew that he was alone apart from the unfortunate and unlamented rat-faced character. He glanced at his watch and screwing the cap back on the flask, quietly moved out of cover and eased towards the cliff edge. He peered over and saw nothing. There was no movement, and no sound but the gentle sough of the morning breeze as it ruffled his dark hair.

Thoughtfully he rubbed his chin, and felt the harshness of new bristles. A shave, a shower and a good meal would be nice, and he wondered idly what they would be doing down below his feet in the tomb. Probably getting up to do all those things. He hoped they'd fed Tornquist, or the man would be having a fit.

At first he thought he was hallucinating, as quite distinctly there came to him, born on the breeze, the smell of bacon and eggs, and just the suggestion of coffee. He shook his head, wondering if his mind was playing tricks and was the subject of wishful thinking; and then he knew it wasn't. The smells were real, and could only mean that someone was cooking breakfast, and an English one at that. There might be herdsmen in the area, drifting slowly after their wandering flocks, but they wouldn't eat that kind of thing even if they could have afforded it. Bacon and egg smells could only be coming from a kitchen somewhere underneath where he stood - and that meant the very air vent he had been hoping for. The fact that he could smell it so clearly meant the breeze was blowing it straight at him, and all he had to do to find it was literally follow his nose and he'd practically fall down the thing.

With infinite patience he once again scanned the area with his binoculars, and seeing nothing, gathered his gear and moved upwind like a grey shadow.

Twenty minutes later, Maxim Gunn was standing at the side of a cleverly concealed air shaft, up which blew a warm stream of bacon scented air, and at that moment he would rather have smelled it than Cynthia Ffoote's Chanel No.5.

He peered over the edge and looked down into the inky depths. Nothing but blackness met his eyes. Nothing to tell him how far it went, whether it was blocked by a grill, if there was a fan waiting to slice him like salami, or where it came out, though reason told him it had to be the kitchen. He shrugged; no use speculating. The only way to find the answers was to go down.

Was this the impossible way in? The area of complacency? Or had it merely been overlooked? No way of knowing. The only thing he was sure of was that he had no better ideas, and no alternative. He took a coil of light nylon rope out of the small rucksack and secured one end round a heavy rock. It was going to be tricky getting down for a couple of reasons, apart from the obvious point of descending into the unknown. One: the air shaft was narrow, barely wider than his shoulders, and once started he would have to keep going, as getting back up would be out of the question. And two: he couldn't let the rope drop as it might end up dangling in front of some cook's startled face - or worse still end up in a cooking fire and start burning. He grinned suddenly at the mental image of himself shinning frantically up with the rope burning after him like a fuse - pure Tom and Jerry stuff. No, he'd have to keep it looped, and pay it out under himself as he went.

He knew he had enough rope, as he'd measured the cliff face by eye and supplied himself accordingly, and without further delay looped the rucksack around his ankle and slid over the edge.

Most men would have spent the time of that descent imagining the worst. Would they make it? Could they keep a grip on the rope with burning hands? When would their screaming arm muscles give up and plummet them into the dark void below? What if...? And they would have died a thousand deaths before accomplishing the task.

Not so Maxim Gunn. He was different, and had a philosophy that would not allow him to think the unthinkable. He shut all thoughts of failure into a locked compartment of his mind, and let his superbly trained muscles get on with the job in hand in automatic mode, while his mind roamed on other problems, one of which was how Wanda had managed to cut the air shaft, and what she had done with the waste material. He knew it was a relatively simple mining problem, carried out regularly all over the world, but Wanda was no miner. He decided her `partners' must have supplied that piece of expertise.

And then his feet touched a ledge, and he allowed himself the luxury of relaxing the tortured muscles in his arms and shoulders. A faint light filtered up towards him, and there was the sound of pans being moved around on a metal stove top, and a man's voice singing tunelessly.

Gunn waited patiently, gathering his strength, until the sounds ceased and he heard a door bang, and guessing that breakfast was over for the time being and the kitchen deserted, he cautiously let himself down the remainder of the shaft.

He ended up, not standing on a stove, as he'd imagined, but in a small alcove behind it, the walls spattered with grease and the floor littered with spilled food. He wondered briefly if Wanda knew the state of her kitchen.

He peered round the corner into the quiet emptiness, and breathed a slow sigh of relief; and then his eyes were drawn as if by magnets to the wooden table in the centre of the room.

Two minutes later he had slapped half a dozen slices of cooling bacon between two slices of bread, swallowed a cup of coffee, and was gently easing open the door. It was amazing how breakfast put a different outlook on the day. He felt ready for anything.

There was no-one outside, and he padded silently down the corridor in the expectation that it would take him to the main part of whatever complex Wanda had usurped for her purposes. There were double doors at the end that looked promising, and as he slowly pushed them open, all hell broke loose with the strident clangour of an alarm bell.

Anyone else would have equalled Ratface's record for the standing high jump, and come to earth quivering like a jelly, but Gunn merely raised an eyebrow and slipped through the door like a wraith, turned sharply right and disappeared behind the first door he came to. He found himself in a distinctly insalubrious bedroom, and by the look of the unmade bed and dirty clothes strewn across the floor, it belonged to the cook.

He sat on the bed after removing a grease spattered apron, and finished the last couple of bites of his sandwich while he thought about this latest development.

He was quite sure no-one had seen him, so the alarm must have been triggered by the opening of the doors. But he hadn't seen any obvious alarm. But then again, he hadn't been looking for one. Maybe he had been a bit complacent himself. He shrugged and licked his fingers, content to wait and see. Maybe they were just having fire drill. If the alarm triggered a room by room search they'd find him anyway, and if not, he'd wait till the ruckus died down.

Gunn was not a fatalist by nature, but he knew there were some occasions when it was better to do nothing than to risk doing the wrong thing.

The Thing settled into the total dark of a part of the tomb no-one had visited in over four thousand years, and was happy. The place was familiar, and in the deep recesses of its evil mind there stirred a memory, indistinct and fragmented, of robed priests and torch light, and blood. And there was sadness in the memory, for such things had passed and were no more. There was still evil in this small, green world, but it was of a different and less dramatic sort. And then it remembered the reason for its coming to the tomb again, and waited as it had waited many times in its limitless life. The woman creature would call again soon, for its help.

Torquil Tornquist woke slowly, feeling groggy and with a splitting headache. He tried to put his hand to his temple to ease the pounding in his skull, and discovered that his arms had been tied to something.

Cautiously he opened his eyes, squinting against the painful light, and blurrily realized he was secured by straps to a chrome plated chair in the centre of a small room, completely blank except for glass windowed doors in front of the chair. He breathed deeply, and then tested the straps, his gigantic muscles straining until the sweat stood out on his forehead, and the seams of his shirt threatened to split. With a low cry of suppressed fury he relaxed and closed his eyes again. It was useless. Then he gathered himself and breathed deeply for a few moments, settling the seething anger and allowing his heart-beat to slow to normal. What now? he thought.

The fact that Wanda Liszt had not immediately ordered a bullet through his brain argued that she had some other delight in store - but what? Or maybe she was simply holding him as a hostage to lure Gunn back.

Anyway, the great thing was the fact that he was still alive, and where there was life there was always hope. And then he laughed quietly to himself, a deep, throaty chuckle that shook his massive frame. He had got inside the tomb, hadn't he, despite the unknown password. And Maxim Gunn was still outside, and that was a plus of more than average proportions. He wondered what Gunn was doing at that moment, and more to the point, whether Wanda Liszt was aware of what he was doing.

Gunn's remarks after the helicopter attack came back with a jolt. Just how had the woman known where to find them so easily in that barren wilderness. Did all the talk of witchcraft, or whatever it was really have some basis after all? Tornquist gave a sharp grunt of anger and switched his mind to the more immediate problem of his surroundings and present predicament. No good wondering about something beyond his control, and possibly beyond anyone's, and certainly no good frightening himself with thoughts of things that went bump in the night.

He chuckled again. Frightened? Torquil Tornquist frightened? Dammit, he wasn't even sure he knew what the word meant.

A faint humming noise came to him through a slight crack in the door, and the odd whirring click of machinery. He frowned, searching for sound recognition, then realized it was a computer, and swore comprehensively, in several languages, at the frustration of being so near and yet so far. Five minutes in there with a wrecking bar, or whatever it was he had been hit on the head with, he thought ruefully, and Wanda could have kissed goodbye to all her mad schemes. And then his eyes followed the cables coming through a conduit from the room beyond, saw they were attached to terminals on the chrome chair, and an icy calm descended on his brain, which was about as near as he would ever come to being alarmed. The evidence was clear that in some way the computer linked with the damned thing; but to do what? It didn't need a high I.Q. to know that whatever it was, he, Tornquist, was not going to enjoy it much.

Time went by. He had no way of knowing how much; but he endured it with a patience that would have amazed Gunn, who had never seen him in anything but a hurry. But Tornquist was an archaeologist, and one did not hurry the unmasking of the secrets of the past. Patience he had in plenty, when required. The one thing troubling him though was his stomach, which kept reminding him uncomfortably that it was a long time since he had last eaten, and he gloomily forecast that it might be a long time till he did again, if ever.

He leant back as comfortably as the chair would allow, and closed his eyes. At least he could build up his reserves of strength for whatever was coming, and there was always the chance that Maxim Gunn would make his presence felt before too long. Torquil Tornquist dozed.

He came to with a slight start as the doors opened and the Baron came into the room and leant silently against the wall. Tornquist looked at him with mild interest, and said.

`A nice little setup you people have here. It's a pity it won't do you any good; though I personally owe you a great debt.'

The Baron raised his eyebrows in surprise, and Tornquist continued. `Without you I would never have got in to the site of the Great Tomb of Gilgamesh. Most gratifying. I thank you.'

The Baron opened his mouth to speak, and then closed it quickly as the sound of quick, angry footsteps was heard. Wanda Liszt threw open the door and stood, legs astride and hands on her hips, her eyes flashing.

`Now, Mr Torquil Tornquist,' she said, harshly. `We shall have to find out how much you and that meddling fool Gunn know.'

Tornquist starred at her in frank admiration. `Now I know I shall enjoy Valhalla,' he said, with a smile. `You will make a perfect Valkyrie.'

Wanda laughed, and turned to the Baron. `Tell the Professor we are ready.'

She lit a cigarette, fitted it into her long silver holder and waved it vaguely. `I imagine you have some idea what this is all about,' she said, blowing a long plume of smoke.

`Enough,' replied the Swede. `Enough to know that you have no chance, and that your little machine will be smashed and you dead before long.'

`You are wrong. This time I shall not fail. However, you will know nothing of the outcome.'

Tornquist managed a disinterested shrug. `I am unimportant, a mere assistant. Others come who will finish the work.'

`Doubtless you refer to Maxim Gunn,' said Wanda, coldly. `He can do nothing against the forces I can muster. Oh, he will come, I have no doubt, out of some misguided sense of loyalty, and attempt your rescue. But I am ready for that. He will be caught, and I shall dispose of him, finally.'

`As well to try and catch the wind,' Tornquist replied.

`We shall see,' Wanda said, and turned to leave. `This little machine, as you call it, will destroy your soul, big man, and render you a mindless zombie.'

`A machine cannot do that.'

Wanda smiled. `This one can. You see, it calls on, shall we say, other things, to aid it.'

Tornquist returned her smile. `What? A demon? A chimera?'

Wanda raised her eyebrows, and replied softly. `Ah, so you do know. Well, let us call it an entity; a force which I control through the computer.'

Tornquist laughed delightedly. `Witchcraft really has caught up with the twentieth century, hasn't it. Fancy using a computer to conjure demons. Have care though, lady. A spell needs a roost, and will come back on the one who casts it if it misses the target.'

`In either case, you will know nothing,' Wanda replied.

Tornquist looked her straight in the eye. `A man can only die once.'

Wanda returned his cool gaze, and wondered what it was about the men she met with Maxim Gunn, and the women. Even when death was inevitable, when escape or rescue was beyond possibility, they did not beg or plead. They met it with a steadiness she could admire, as the man Henderson had.

`Before you go,' Tornquist said. `Tell me one thing. Is this really the Tomb of Gilgamesh?'

Wanda nodded. `It is.'

Tornquist sighed. `Then I am happy. I go in good company.'

Before she could stop herself, Wanda Liszt raised a hand in a short salute, swung on her heel, and left the room. The door closed softly behind her with a slight hiss.

Tornquist waited. He felt strangely at ease, quite curious and certainly not afraid. His one regret was that he might not be the one to reveal the secrets of the tomb to the outside world. His other thought was to wonder if Maxim Gunn would be on time. He was cutting it very short.

In the computer room Wanda stood in the pentagram, touched the keyboard of the terminal with a few deft strokes, and waited.

The Thing felt the woman creature's call, and stirred, this time with more interest, as it felt there was a different reason. It moved its primitive mind forward in response to the call and the commands; searching, reaching for the target, and through the electronic maze of the computer, came to Tornquist's brain. Its mind tentacles probed cautiously as it encountered fierce resistance, and it chuckled wetly, and pushed.

Quite suddenly Tornquist felt a tingling sensation run across his scalp, which quickly turned to pain as something seemed to burrow like a white hot worm. He struggled against the straps, and mouthed obscenities in an effort to concentrate, but it was no use. A wild, vicious lance of pain ripped through his temples, and his eyes went out of focus. It was as if his mind was being sucked clean by a vacuum pump. Flashes of agony pierced the last lingering remains of consciousness as he arched his back, mouth open in a soundless shriek that was part pain and part horror at what he saw and felt. And then it was over. Blackness. Nothing. Oblivion, and his limp body slumped like a rag doll against the chrome chair.

Some minutes later Wanda's face appeared at the window, and she gave his unconscious form a look of satisfaction. She had learned little, but had further demonstrated to herself and the thoroughly frightened Baron, that her powers were real. Some obtained obedience from their followers by example, some by reward, and some by fear. Wanda preferred the last method. It gave her greater pleasure. She turned away with a cruel smile, and Tornquist was left in silence.

Gunn glanced at his watch, judged that enough time had elapsed to rule out a search, and was about to get off the rumpled bed when he heard a door bang and heavy footsteps approach. He slipped behind the door, and waited.

The cook came into the room, went to a steel locker beside the bed and taking out a bottle of what looked like whisky, uncorked it, and was about to put it to his lips when he caught sight of Gunn out of the corner of his eye. His half-formed cry of alarm stayed half formed as Gunn's hand caught him a sharp-edged blow below the ear, and he buckled at the knees. Gunn caught the bottle, and the cook before they both hit the ground, and lowered them soundlessly. He looked at the label on the bottle and shuddered delicately. Some people had about as much taste as a vulture, and at that time of day too.

Quickly he searched the locker for a reasonably clean white overall and chef's hat, put them on, carefully opened the door and sneaked a look into the passage outside. It was all clear, and keeping his head lowered, he set off to look for Tornquist, or Wanda, or anyone else who happened to be around. It was time to start something happening.

He followed the passage to another set of double doors, pushed through rather carelessly as if he had a perfect right to be there, and made to sidestep the man who was standing guard on the other side. He had a machine pistol at the ready.

Gunn mumbled something indistinct, and keeping his head down, started to move on.

`Just a minute, friend,' came a gravelly voice from the guard. Gunn doubted if he was ever likely to be the man's friend, stopped as if uncertain it was he being called, and half turned. The guard took three quick steps, his weapon levelled, and was about to shout when Gunn's right leg shot out in a flying kick under the man's jaw and he ceased to have any further interest in anyone's identity.

Gunn stooped quickly to pick up the fallen weapon, and then froze as a new voice said. `No, Mr Gunn. Leave it exactly where it is. We don't know where it's been, do we.'

Gunn straightened slowly as he recognized the voice, and turned. `Well, well. If it isn't the dear old Baron,' he said casually. `And what's a nasty fellow like you doing in a nice tomb like this?'

CHAPTER SIXTEEN

The weapon the Baron was pointing directly at Gunn's stomach quickly killed any thoughts he might have had of taking a chance. Even the world's worst shot couldn't have missed at that range with a Savage 77E combat shotgun, and the Baron was a very good shot. Gunn raised his hands without being told, and moved in the direction indicated. They were quickly joined by another guard, heartlessly leaving the other to come to in his own time.

`You'll let me know when I'm getting warm,' said Gunn.

`Stop chattering,' snapped the Baron. `Go slowly through those doors to your right, and then stop.'

Gunn did as he was told, and seconds later stopped, very suddenly, with the inevitable result that the guard got too close before realizing his mistake. His machine pistol clattered to the floor and he yelled in pain as Gunn broke his wrist with a lightning attack. Uncharacteristically he did not pursue his advantage, but merely murmured. `Another redskin bites the dust. I wonder how many there are to go.' Then he sauntered through the doors, into the room, and looked around. He raised his eyebrows at the shambles Tornquist had made of Wanda's sitting room, and said.

`Really, Baron. I know it's hard to get good help these days, but this is ridiculous.' Then he saw Wanda glaring at him balefully and gave her a mocking bow. `Wanda, light of my life. You must have more lives than a cat.'

`Which is more than I can say for you, Gunn. You've already used up three, and this is the final one. This time there will be no mistake, and I shall be rid of your interfering for good.'

Gunn managed to look disappointed. `Sounds dreadfully serious. What is it to be this time. A pit full of cobras? A cup of hemlock? Or is the Baron just going to bore me to death?'

`You will find out soon enough, and it won't be pleasant.'

`Oh well,' Gunn sighed. `We who are about to die, and all that. But at least the gladiators had a chance.'

`You will have none,' Wanda snapped.

`So you keep on saying,' Gunn replied. `And yet, here I am, large as life. What happened here, by the way? The secondhand value of the furniture seems to have dropped a bit.'

`Your friend, Tornquist, took advantage of my guard's carelessness. But he has been restrained, and will shortly cease to bother anyone ever again.'

Gunn laughed. `Yes, he does get a bit boisterous on occasion. I've had to speak to him about it once before. I suppose that means you won't be able to ask me to sit down and enjoy your company, but never mind, I have a feeling you weren't going to anyway.'

`Quite right,' Wanda answered shortly. `In fact, the Baron was about to take you away.' The Baron moved, shotgun at the ready, but Gunn held up his hand. `Satisfy my curiosity on one point before he does. How did you get away from the Schloss?'

The Baron threw Wanda an uneasy glance, but she replied simply. `I had help.'

`Must have been the devil,' said Gunn, quietly. `I personally dropped the best part of a mountain on you. It was quite a bang,' he added, with pride.

Wanda remained impassive. `There are more things in heaven and earth...'

`Than I know of? Quite probably. But I think in this case you mean hell.'

Wanda's eyes narrowed. `What does that mean?'

`Merely that we understand each other. Take care, Wanda. I think you're dabbling in something that's liable to get out of control.'

Wanda Liszt shrugged, turned away to get a cigarette, lit it and said. `Enough of this nonsense. Take him away, Baron. You know what to do.'

The Thing stirred in the darkness of its lair. It sensed there was another person in the tomb, one inimical to it, but with a familiar aura. There was something about the new arrival which it did not like, and it stirred with discomfort, even fear. The man thing had a point of light in the centre near its life-force; something it could not touch. It growled uneasily, and the fear was surmounted by anger.

Gunn's mind was racing as the squad marched him off down the rock-hewn passages, and he felt he knew what the inmates of the Tower of London had gone through as they went to the block. Any attempt to escape right then would have been met with a hail of bullets before he had gone a couple of strides, and was out of the question. The thing to do was wait and see; and opportunity would present itself. One thing he was sure of, it would be real cordon bleu stuff. Wanda simply didn't have it in her to pull a trigger and be done with it; she had to think up something special, and that's where his chance would lie. Once again, he wondered briefly what Tornquist was doing, or what they had done to him after the wrecking episode.

They came to the bottom of a long, sloping descent, and stopped in front of a massive arch blocked by a stone slab on which were carved groups of symbols that were meaningless to Gunn. He thought the Swede would have figured them out in a moment, and a twinge of conscience made him think he might be acting a bit too casually towards his new friend. Then he pushed the thought away.

One problem at a time; and problem number one was to get free and in a position to do something practical.

The Baron pressed two of the groups of symbols, Gunn noted carefully which ones, and the slab moved ponderously aside to reveal a dark cavernous emptiness. Gunn peered interestedly inside. `Ali Baba's cave, I imagine,' he said. `We've certainly got the forty thieves, anyway. What now?'

`Your description is more accurate than you think,' the Baron replied. `It was the treasure room of Gilgamesh, and I might add the treasure is no longer in it.'

`Grave robbers?'

`No. A spin off, you might say. There are museums that will pay highly for such things.'

`And to hell with knowledge and history,' Gunn murmured.

`Precisely,' said the Baron with a thin smile. `But, as you will shortly discover, the builders installed some very effective anti-burglar devices. Now, if you please.' And he waved Gunn into the opening.

The guards weapons made any argument worse than useless, and Gunn stepped forward cautiously, sniffing the air. At least it smelled fresh, and he wasn't liable to asphyxiate at once.

`Go ahead, Mr Gunn,' the Baron urged. `The safety devices are not activated until the slab is back in position, and to be pushed would be so undignified.'

`How considerate,' Gunn replied. `Ah well, don't wait up for me; this may take a little time.' And with a flick of the fingers he went inside, then stood rock still as the slab ground back into place, every sense fine-tuned to the first hint of danger.

Just what had the Baron meant by anti-burglar devices? The builders having installed them ruled out anything alive, so there'd be no pits full of cobras, no sudden attacks by ravenous beasts. Then what? Pitfalls, drop bars? He hadn't a clue. He was just going to have to be very, very careful; and very quick. But first things first. He took out a gas lighter that had been among his small collection of tools, wondering briefly why he hadn't been searched, and holding the small, flickering flame above his head, peered into the gloom. There was nothing to see but more darkness, and far to one side the vague shapes of rough hewn rock.

Torquil Tornquist groaned and moved against the straps securing him as consciousness returned slowly to his tortured mind. He grunted like a confused bear surfacing from hibernation and shook his massive, bearded head to try and clear the almost overpowering muzziness. Where was he? What had happened?

For several minutes nothing made sense, and then, slowly, he began to remember. His eyes widened and he twitched, veins starting on his forehead, as the horror of his encounter with the Creature returned. He had looked into the very pit of hell; had fought with one of the devil's own creations, and knew that were it to come again, he would be lost.

This time however, he had somehow won; he had fought off the attack; and even as his mind raged with the visions conjured from his subconscious, he began to calm, and his massive will and Herculean strength reasserted themselves.

Tornquist lifted his shaggy head and roared defiance at the empty room, and then, as if purged by the challenge, he calmed, straightened himself, and a slow smile spread across his face. Dammit, and by all the Gods of his fathers, he would not let these people defeat him, and he would not be dragged down by whatever nameless thing had invaded his brain. Next time he would be ready.

He, Torquil Tornquist, had not even begun to fight.

Realizing his best offense would be surprise, he

relaxed his body and mind, and allowed his inner strength to take over; breathing slowly and evenly as he had once been taught by an advanced practitioner of yoga.

Time passed without him being aware of its passing, and only came back into focus when he heard footsteps approaching. He feigned unconsciousness and waited, hardly breathing, and coiled like a monstrous spring about to explode.

The doors opened and two men came in to inspect him. One of them said in a voice of mingled satisfaction and contempt.

`It's like she said it would be. Take off the straps and we'll get him outside - ready for the high dive.'

The other man sniggered. `The bigger they are, eh? This one'll go just like the other. Three hundred feet - and bang.'

`Yea. It was like pushing a drunk off. Now give me a hand.'

Tornquist felt their hands fumble at the straps on his wrists and ankles. The straps fell away and rough hands began to lift him, and at that moment he exploded with all the pent up rage, frustration and humiliation he had suffered. He locked his huge arms around their necks, and before either could make a sound, smashed their heads together. There was a woody thud, and the men dropped like poleaxed beasts. They never knew what hit them.

Tornquist reached the door in one long stride, and looked through the glass. There was one man, hunched over the computer key-board, entering data. As Tornquist watched he straightened, looked at his watch and then at the door behind which the Swede lurked. He frowned, got up, and went to it.

As Professor Shrinkker pushed through the doors and saw the two guards stretched out like rag dolls, his gasp was quickly choked off as Tornquist's huge hand closed like a vice around his throat, and he was lifted off his feet.

The giant barged into the computer room carrying his prize at arm's length, shaking the man roughly in time to his words.

`Though shalt not suffer nasty, mad little scientists to live. Thus sayeth Torquil Tornquist. And you, Edouard Shrinkker, are a very nasty, mad little scientist; and I am going to smash you into little pieces along with your diabolical machine.'

Shrinkker's face by that time had turned an interesting shade of purple, and he was obviously having a great deal of difficulty in breathing as he struggled futilely, trying to kick and claw at Tornquist's legs and hands.

Still holding him securely in one massive hand, Tornquist wadded some sheets of printout and stuffed them in his mouth, and then, ripping a length of cable that snaked from the console, bound his hands and legs like a trussed turkey. Shrinkker made one last attempt to kick his captor, got smartly tapped on the head for his pains, and promptly ceased to have any further interest in the proceedings.

Tornquist looked down at the crumpled heap of humanity at his feet, shrugged, and began looking for a convenient tool to start his wrecking operation. Someone more expert in the expensive equipment before him could probably have inserted a bug in the programme, given time, or wiped it from the computer memory; but Tornquist was no expert; in fact his knowledge of computers extended about as far as using a pocket calculator. But one thing he did know, and it was that an enthusiastically applied hammer, or something equivalent, didn't do them any good at all. His eyes lit on a heavy steel office chair, and he was just about to bring it crashing onto the console for starters, when the door burst open and two more guards came in.

They had just enough time to register that all was not going quite as planned, when the chair hit the leading guard in the chest like a cannon-ball, and he staggered back, treading heavily on the man behind. Tornquist bellowed like an enraged bull and rushed them. His charge carried the pair through the doors and into the passage outside, where they hit the wall with bone jarring force and slid limply down it with vacant eyes.

Having substantially reduced the opposing forces, he set off in the general direction of where he supposed the living quarters to be. Tornquist knew nothing of Gunn's problem, and in fact didn't even know he had got into the tomb; he was motivated purely by revenge, and simply intent on doing something unpleasant to Wanda Liszt and the Baron.

Halfway along the passage he found what he wanted, a pair of doors that looked familiar, and nearly took them off the hinges as he smashed through; and then skidded to a stop as he was confronted by Wanda, the Baron and Auntie de Lorian, all with very serviceable firearms pointed directly at his chest.

Tornquist was a practical man however, and masked his disappointment as he momentarily weighed his chances; then, totally ignoring the Baron's automatic, he pushed him to one side, made for the sideboard and poured himself half a glass of neat brandy. He swallowed and breathed a sigh of pure pleasure.

`Exercise always makes me thirsty,' he said, and hooking an unbroken chair towards himself with his foot, sat down heavily astride it, arms folded across the back.

`What now, my little ones?' he asked.

Wanda was the first to recover from the shock of his entry. The Swede's sudden appearance had thrown her off balance as she had assumed he was by then safely on his way to the cliff top and about to take a long dive.

`If you've come looking for Gunn,' she said, `you're too late.'

`You mean he left without saying good-bye?' Tornquist

replied, looking disappointed. Inwardly he was delighted. Gunn had made it into the tomb after all, and that meant that however they both might be temporarily halted, Wanda had her hands full.

`He returned,' Wanda continued. `No doubt with some misguided idea of rescuing you. Unfortunately for him he was careless, and left one of my guards still alive on the cliff top. The man was discovered at the change of shift.'

`Yes,' Tornquist replied, sadly. `Gunn's like that. He doesn't seem to think it much fun to kill people unnecessarily, unlike you. Anyway, I suppose you know what you're talking about as I certainly don't. Where is he, by the way; or is that a secret?'

`No secret, Mr Tornquist. Gunn is at present in what used to be the treasure chamber of this place. As an archaeologist you possibly know something of the quaint, but effective mechanical devices the ancients used for protecting their valuables. Gunn is no doubt making firsthand acquaintance with those ingenious toys right now.' She smiled, and Tornquist saw she was actually enjoying the thought. It made him all the more determined to see she came to as permanent an end as possible, but the thought made his blood run cold. Outwardly he remained calm, and indeed he held out his empty glass to the Baron, who was so mesmerized that he refilled it.

`No problem,' he said. `After four thousand odd years, none of them will work.'

`On the contrary,' Wanda replied, smiling even more broadly. `We know one of them still does. It has been tried.'

CHAPTER SEVENTEEN

Gunn took an exploratory pace forward - it was the only way to go, and it was only his lightning reaction and superb physical agility that saved him from plummeting down the shaft which opened at his feet, as a slight movement telegraphed itself to his brain and he leapt sideways and watched with respect as the ancient mechanism returned the slab into position with a slight thud. His lighter continued to flicker and cast weird shadows on the rock walls.

There was possibly another way out, some other trigger for the door in case the priests who had tended the place originally shut themselves in by mistake. Or was there? Maybe they simply ended up as offerings to the gods. It was not a pleasant thought. At any rate, he had to make the effort, or starve to death. All of which meant moving around the treasure room, and no doubt setting off some other nasty surprises. To say that he was going to have to be careful was the understatement of all time.

He slid his feet cautiously forward along the stone floor, the lighter held high for maximum effect, the feeble flame giving no more than a few feet of poor light. Half a dozen slow, measured paces; senses alert for the slightest message, the first hint of danger not so much seen or heard, but felt by his highly tuned sixth sense. Nothing. So far so good. And then he saw the dark stain of dried blood, barely discernible on the rough floor, just in time to throw himself flat as the huge rusty blade slashed from the roof, powered by God knew what, and sang inches over his head. Gunn thought that the poor devil who had found the place could never have known what hit him.

He began to make his way slowly back to the

entrance, re-tracing his steps. At least he knew the problem in that direction, and if there was another means of opening the place, logic said it would be there.

Near the door, he saw an ancient rushlight fixed to the wall in a rotting copper bracket, a relic of more than four thousand years and no doubt priceless from an archaeologist's point of view; but he had no time for sentiment, ripped it from the flimsy fastening, and lit it. The result was a considerable improvement, and within seconds the air was filled with the smells of incense and burning pitch.

There was air enough in the chamber to last indefinitely, or at least longer than he would without food or drink, so there was no need to go off half-cocked. He eased himself to the floor, and the flaming torch in his hand reminded him of Tornquist. So much for rescue attempts, he thought, wryly. He'd be flat out getting himself out of this mess without thinking of others at the moment; and no doubt the Swede was big enough and ugly enough to look after himself. Not for the first time he thought of the stupidity of involving amateurs in games like this. Wanda Liszt, for all her criminal ruthlessness, was professional. There were risks which she accepted as part of the business, just as he did; but Tornquist had gone in blind, almost in a spirit of adventure as if the penalties were no more than a slap on the wrist if caught. Gunn knew they weren't. The penalties had a tendency to be permanent.

Then he held the flame down to his watch, and looked at the time almost automatically before realizing that time had no real meaning. Suddenly his mind snapped to attention. The flame was wavering. Wavering flames meant a draught, and draughts didn't blow through solid rock. The air had to be going to, or coming from somewhere; and that could mean a way out if he could find it without being clubbed, stabbed, chopped in half or otherwise slowed down - and if the exit was big enough for more than a rat.

He stood up, brushed the dust from his trousers automatically, and wetting his finger to get the direction of the draught, set off carefully across the chamber. Never say die, he thought, and certainly not when he was around. There was a way out, because there had to be. He was not going to die in this stinking dusty deathtrap of an old tomb just to satisfy Wanda Liszt's lust for vengeance.

He skirted the place where the knife blade trigger lurked, took another couple of careful paces, when the slight creak of ancient machinery sent alarm bells clanging in his head. He threw himself sideways with a quick prayer to the gods of battle that it was the right way, and was just in time to avoid the three heavy spear shafts that hissed over his shoulder and clattered in the darkness against the far wall.

Slowly he got up and massaged a bruised knee. This was definitely not going to do. Sooner or later his luck was going to run out. Of course, sooner or later the surprises were going to run out too, but it was a toss up which would happen first, and he didn't like the odds. At least, he thought, there'd be nothing that crept, or slithered, or bit or stung. He knew of no species that could have survived that long without food - unless there were more than one species and they fed on each other, and unless Wanda had put something in there to liven up the entertainment.

Gunn was afraid of no natural thing. It was not in his make up. He had no phobias about snakes or tarantulas for instance. There was nothing that lived on earth, or in the water with which he felt he couldn't cope. But what of Termaxian's fears? What of Vileman's suspicions? If there was any basis to those, and there might be, then perhaps he did have something to fear. Maybe there was something so far outside his experience; so far from the natural world, that if he was confronted by it he would not know what to do. He remembered Tornquist's quote from Madame Curie that the unknown was not to be feared, only understood, and as his fingers touched the silver amulet at his neck, he once again felt the strange comfort from it.

Still, he had no option. To stay still was to die another way, lingeringly, of hunger and thirst. He moved off again.

Tornquist took another sip of brandy, raised his right hand to scratch the back of his neck, and his fingers touched the bone handle of the knife tucked in its sheath under his collar. Experience in lonely parts of the world, where the law tended to be sparse or what you made it, had taught him that a concealed weapon could be useful. His fingers tightened on the haft, and, with a powerful flick of the wrist, he sent the keen blade spinning at the Baron, at the same time ducking sideways.

The Baron yelled with shock as the knife bit into his shoulder. He dropped his machine pistol and clawed at the pain. Wanda stared at him in open-mouthed surprise, and was in the act of swinging her own gun back to the Swede, when with a roar, he leapt across the room, slapping Auntie de Lorian aside as he did so, and grabbed Wanda from her seat. He tucked her under his arm, and was out of the door and into the corridor before she had time to shout. She started to wriggle. He clamped his hand over her mouth, and was promptly bitten. Annoyed, he cuffed her lightly with his free hand and she went still. He swore at himself in irritation as he needed her to tell him where the Treasure Room was.

Yells from de Lorian and the Baron came strongly to him, and he knew he had only seconds before the remaining guards were alerted; and again he wondered how many were left.

Rounding a corner like a runaway locomotive, he barged into a man clutching a revolver. The collision knocked this unfortunate off his feet, and Tornquist collected his unconscious form under his other arm. Only one more, he thought, and I'll have a set.

He kicked open a door and barged in. The room inside was empty, and dropping Wanda unceremoniously on the floor, he turned his attention to the guard, who was starting to come round. He slapped the man none too gently to get his attention, and said.

`I shall only ask once. Hesitate, and both you and the lady will die. Where is the Treasure Room?'

The man tried to struggle, but he might as well have been fighting a four hundred pound gorilla as Tornquist's massive hand clamped round his head, and squeezed. His prisoner squealed like a trapped rabbit, and frantically told him. Tornquist nodded, tapped him on the jaw, and the man sagged like a puppet with cut strings.

Tornquist scooped Wanda up again, tucked her under his arm, and tightened his grip as she began struggling. A string of very unpleasant names came from her lips.

`Hush, my lovely,' Tornquist commanded. `Time for the sweet talk when we are alone, later. Right now we have business to attend to. Maxim Gunn must be freed.'

The foul language continued until he was forced to clamp his hand over her mouth again, reducing her to inarticulate mumbling.

Within seconds he was standing in front of the archway with its frieze of hieroglyphics. He set Wanda on her feet and asked.

`The door. How do I open it? Don't force me to hurt you.'

Wanda spat at him in fury. He tightened the arm that was circling her shoulders, and she cried out, but refused to answer.

`No matter,' he laughed. `I almost forgot. I am an

archaeologist, aren't I, and should be able to read those funny squiggles.' And he began to examine the carved message, moving his lips silently as he said the words of the long dead language. Then he laughed, and said, wonderingly. `You wouldn't believe it, but I actually can read the stuff.' And he leant forward, hand outstretched. `Now, if I just follow instructions and press here, oh, and here of course, it should ...'

The slab moved sideways with a grating rumble, and keeping a tight hold on his hostage, Tornquist peered through the dark opening and shouted. `Come on, Maxim. Time to stop playing silly games. We've got work to do, and our little friend here wants to say goodbye.'

Gunn whirled with relieved surprise, saw the huge silhouette in the opening, and replied. `Not another step, Torquil. This place is booby trapped to hell and gone.'

`Not any more it isn't.'

`What does that mean?'

`I've put the safety catch on.' He smiled at Wanda. `You didn't know about that, did you.'

`If you're telling me lies,' said Gunn.

`You won't do anything, Maxim. You'll be dead. Now get a move on.' His face brightened as a thought struck him. `Look, I'll prove it.' And with that he shoved Wanda through the opening and she skidded to a stop, rigid, mouth open.

`Now do you believe me?'

Nothing happened, so Gunn shrugged, tossed the flaming torch into a corner, and as he passed her on the way out she made a desperate grab to stop him, clawing at his arm. There were words in her eyes that he knew she could never bring herself to say. He brushed her off, and she fell to the floor. He felt no mercy, but his words were light. `We've got to stop meeting in places like this. It's giving me a bad name.'

Tornquist pulled him through the door, and then turned

to Wanda, who was recovering her poise. `I am going to close the door,' he said. `But this time you will be on the receiving end, and only I shall know whether the catch is on or off.' And then he pressed the catch on the outside wall. As the slab began to rumble into place, Wanda scrambled to her feet and ran frantically to the narrowing opening; but she was too late. It closed with a dull thud, and they heard her despairing cry. Gunn looked at Tornquist speculatively, and asked.

`Is it?'

`Is what?'

`Is the catch on or off?'

`What catch?' Tornquist replied, with a huge laugh.

`You mean to tell me there isn't one, and I just walked across that damned floor. Do you know what's in there?'

`Well, you got out, didn't you? And I can imagine.'

`But Wanda .. why didn't she...?'

`Just luck, I guess.'

Tornquist put a ham-like hand on his shoulder. `Some time ago, in Ankara, you told me there was no need to bring these people to the police, and I believed you. Now I know it. They are utterly evil, and she is the worst of them. They deserve no mercy. Now, come, my friend, we must get out of this place; but before we do there is just one bit of this ancient writing I want to look at again more closely.'

Gunn leant casually against the wall as if they had all the time in the world. `There are a couple of things against that,' he said, mildly. `You've just stirred this place up like a stick poked into a hornet's nest. Their fearless leader, Wanda Liszt, is in that room - though they don't know it yet; but there might just be one or two people looking for her, and I expect you've done various other sorts of damage recently, to judge by the look of the drawing room when I last saw it. Don't you think we ought to get moving. After all, we've got a computer to destroy, and a mad scientist to shut up, just in case you've forgotten.'

`I have not forgotten, my friend,' Tornquist replied.

`And there'll be plenty of time to study that writing when you come back here, covered in fame and fortune.'

Tornquist shook his head, a trifle sadly Gunn thought. `No, I don't think so. Please bear with me.' He bent forward, and looking closely at the hieroglyphics, gave a small grunt of satisfaction.

`Ah, yes. It is as I thought.' Then he straightened and ran a hand through his shaggy hair. `Well, everything else seems to work perfectly, so I don't see why that shouldn't too.' He smiled at Gunn. `Now we can go.'

Gunn hitched himself off the wall. `Thank you. And what was all that about?'

`You'll see,' Tornquist replied, mysteriously, and with that same trace of sadness in his voice. `Trust me.'

Gunn's instincts led him unerringly to the computer room, with Tornquist trailing behind like a great, shambling bear. They pushed through the door, and Gunn stopped in surprise when he saw the Professor, still trussed and gagged.

`Your handiwork I presume,' he said, mildly.

`Oh, I forgot about him,' replied the Swede. `There was a little trouble here some time ago.'

Gunn turned and saw the two guards, still unconscious, and the bent metal chair. `So I see. Any more of those?'

Tornquist shrugged disinterestedly. `There are two more in the little room over there, but I think maybe they will not bother us again. I was angry,' he added by way of excuse.

Gunn nodded, understandingly. `Now, from my experience of computers - which, by the way, is not as good as I would like it to be ...'

`Better than mine,' Tornquist interrupted.

`All you have to do,' Gunn continued smoothly, `to send this baby out of its electronic mind, thus wrecking it beyond repair, is to ...'

`No need for any of that,' Tornquist cut in. `It is all going to be taken care of: the computer, the Professor, Wanda, everything. As I said; trust me.'

Gunn looked at his companion for a long moment, weighing him up, and then nodded. `Whatever it is you've got up your sleeve must pack a pretty solid punch. O.K. I trust you. What now? Do we just leave?'

`We get to the main entrance first. You keep me covered for a couple of minutes, and then, well, we get the hell out of it as quickly as possible.'

`I see,' replied Gunn, politely. `Well, let's go. Have a care though; there might be a few people looking for us.'

`Then that will be their fault,' Tornquist replied, bluntly.

CHAPTER EIGHTEEN

The Thing felt the shock transmitted from Wanda Liszt as the stone slab closed on her. It felt her anger and her fear, and knew that something was wrong; but there was no communication in the way it had become accustomed to. The machine was sending no message, and in the absence of instruction it sent out a mind probe, searching for the woman creature that was its earthly self. It found her, and knew what it had to do.

Gunn and Tornquist were halfway to the door when they realized they had left it too late, as the sounds of shouting and running feet told them there was a search party outside. The door slammed open and the Baron ran in, followed by Auntie de Lorian, her grey hair hanging untidily, and two more guards. They were all armed, Gunn and Tornquist were not.

The Baron, his injured arm tucked into his jacket for support and looking grey-faced with pain, took one sweeping glance at the scene and levelled his weapon. The guards fanned out, their machine pistols covering the two men. De Lorian saw the Professor, and going quickly to him, began to untie the cords. Gunn saw the Baron's finger tighten on the trigger as he croaked, harshly. `Where is Madame Liszt?'

Gunn looked at Tornquist, questioningly, and receiving a shrug in reply, said. `I'm not quite sure, but we left her in the Treasure Room.'

Auntie de Lorian looked up quickly as she undid the last knot, and the Professor groaned with returning consciousness. `What? She's in there? We must get her out.'

`Probably too late,' Gunn replied. `I said I knew where

she was; not where she is now. I nearly fell down one hole, and I've no idea where that went to. Perhaps she wasn't so quick.'

The Baron made the mistake of taking his eyes off them to issue an order to one of the guards, and in that second Tornquist swept the battered steel chair off the floor and hurled it. It caught the Baron on the shins, sweeping him off his feet and forcing a cry of agony from him as he jarred his wounded shoulder.

The guards, with no orders to follow, and not knowing whether they should shoot, hesitated fractionally, and that was their mistake. Tornquist launched himself like a shell from a naval gun, swept the first one off his feet and hurled him against the far wall, where he hung limply for a moment; and then slid, lifelessly to the floor.

Auntie de Lorian grabbed for the revolver she had laid down when tending to the Professor, but she was too late. Maxim Gunn's arm snaked out with the speed of a striking cobra, and scooping it from beneath her hand, he levelled it at her heart. There was no mistaking the message in his eyes, and she slowly retreated, spitting hate and defiance.

The second guard decided discretion was the better part of valour and elected to stay alive. He dropped his machine pistol and raised his hands. The Professor, his wits slowly returning, staggered groggily to his feet and looked dazedly about, and then slumped dejectedly as the situation became clear.

`And now can we go?' asked Gunn, mildly.

Tornquist was puzzled for a second, and then laughed. `Yes, my friend, this time we go. And keep me covered a little better this time.'

In the Treasure Room, Wanda Liszt had not moved since Gunn had left with his mocking farewell. She knew nothing of the dangers of the place, except that they were very real, and had caused the death of one of her men. The ancient torch still guttered feebly a dozen feet from her against the wall, but she did not dare get it for fear of setting off one of the death traps. Silently she raged, unable to do anything to help herself, and yet knowing she must remain calm. Gunn had stayed alive; and if he could do it, so could she. And like him, she knew there had to be a way out.

And then she felt the Thing's anger, and despite her awful situation, smiled. She had no control over what she knew was about to happen - but then, neither had Maxim Gunn.

Gunn took one last regretful look at the computer, wishing there was time to smash it, and then turned to follow Tornquist, and in doing so, cannoned into the giant, who was standing, rooted to the spot like a granite statue.

`What the hell ...?' he began.

`Get into the pentagram,' Tornquist roared, and for the first time Gunn detected fear in his friend's voice. `If you value your life and sanity, get into the pentagram.'

Momentarily shocked by the intensity of the command, Gunn followed the Swede's rigid gaze, and felt the hairs on the back of his neck raise.

An unearthly red, shimmering light seemed to come from an unseen source, and it was not a kindly glow; there was something evil about it, and it pulsed, gathering strength with each second. And then, in the semi darkness by the wall hangings with their cabalistic signs, a darker shape loomed mistily. Even as he watched, the outline hardened and solidified, until it assumed a vaguely human form - but what a human. Its black, scaly body was the height and build of a standing gorilla; long, powerful arms hung bowed from massive hunched shoulders, ending in huge clawed hands, and what head there was to see against the shadowy background, seemed to grow out of the shoulders without a neck. But it was the creature's eyes that held his attention, and made his heart beat ever so slightly faster. The eyes were red, glowing like hot coals, and throbbed as if throwing out an unseen power.

`Don't look at the eyes,' Tornquist shouted urgently. `Whatever you do, don't look at the eyes. And for God's sake get into the pentagram.'

Pentagram? thought Gunn. What the hell is a pentagram? And then he remembered the five pointed figure on the floor, and half-forgotten folklore tumbled back into his mind. Inside the pentagram you were supposed to be safe from the powers of evil. It made sense. He dragged his eyes from the awful thing against the wall, feeling its insistent command, and took a strained step back before realizing Tornquist would be outside the pentagram's magical protection.

`You too,' he shouted, hoarsely, as a feeling of cold fear struck him for the first time in his life. `Come with me.'

Tornquist either ignored him, or did not hear, and Gunn reached out and grabbed his arm. The giant turned, wild eyed as fear attacked him too, and was about to lash out, when he shook his head dazedly in recognition, nodded, and stumbled after him. They reached the silver inlaid figure just as the creature gained its full solid form. The black scaled body rippled and glistened in the red light as the muscles in its gigantic arms flexed, and the clawed fingers hooked forward, searching for living prey. Gunn was sickened by the ropes of thick saliva that dropped from its gaping, fanged mouth.

Out of the corner of his eye he caught a momentary glimpse of the others in the chamber, forgotten in the terrifying chain of events that was taking place. The old woman, De Lorian, was crawling, whimpering feebly in abject terror; trying to hide herself under the computer console. Professor Shrinkker, primarily responsible for the conjuring of the frightful thing that had materialized, was on his knees, hands clutching his chest as spasms shook him; and the unfortunate guard, no more than a pawn, a hired hand with no control or knowledge of what was happening, was standing, hands outstretched beseechingly, trying to ward off the horror he could not understand.

`What the hell is it?' Gunn breathed, as an awful stench hit him, making him gag. Never in his life had he smelled anything as totally dreadful. It reeked of death and long dead things.

Tornquist shook his head, confused. `I don't know exactly. A fiend from Hell maybe, but it's the thing our friend Wanda has been controlling. It's what she's been getting her power from.'

`Can it be stopped?'

`Now, yes, I think so. But let it get worse - or rather let her get worse - and I don't think anyone will. She'll be too powerful.'

`She?'

`Yes. I think that thing is somehow a manifestation of her dark side,' Tornquist replied, and Gunn could hear the tones of the scholar creeping into his voice, despite the danger.

`I didn't know she had a light one,' he said, sourly.

`Everyone has a dark side, Maxim. Normally our two natures: good and evil, dark and light, stay apart mostly, with only occasional exchanges. But I think, when she came back from wherever she went when she `died', that thing came back with her. So far I think they are only using each other. But if they become one, who knows what might happen.'

`What if she dies?' Gunn asked, thinking of the Treasure Room.

Tornquist shrugged. `I think it will dissipate. It cannot survive alone. Its existence has to be symbiotic, as part of something else. There must be a balance.'

And then, without warning, the creature launched itself at them with a roaring scream of fury. The malevolence in its eyes was red hot, and Gunn staggered as a bolt of pure hate, solid as a fist, struck him in the chest, aimed at the amulet.

`Stay in the pentagram,' Tornquist shouted, hoarsely. `Whatever happens, don't leave. Don't let it get to you.'

Gunn regained his balance, shook his head to clear it, and reached inside his shirt for Termaxian's parting gift. He ripped his shirt open and held the silver amulet out, forcing the creature to see it.

It staggered as if struck, and then retreated a step or two, fangs bared and hissing throatily. Gunn stood rock still, willing himself to feel no fear.

`What do we do now?' he asked, almost conversationally.

`Call for the Light,' came the reply. `It will give you strength to fight this thing.'

`And how do I do that?' Gunn asked, with a humourless smile. `I can't throw a damned switch.'

`Think light. Think strength. Think love. Think the colour blue - and feel them all.'

Gunn had a momentary blank; the mental switch was too great. And then his survival instinct asserted itself at full strength, and he thought, concentrating as never before.

All his life he had faced odds, sometimes beyond reasonable hope; and always he had won out, managed to beat them. But then he had faced things he could take on with fist and boot, gun and knife and brains. They had been physical things of this earth, and understood. The lowering, dark, malevolent entity facing them was something else, and his only protection a five pointed figure inlaid in the floor under his feet, and a silver bauble on a chain around his neck. It was beyond his experience. But Tornquist had said that to win he had to think light, and strength, and love - and think them he did.

Maxim Gunn concentrated his whole being on winged angels, and wild galloping white horses; on sunlight through country church windows, and children's laughter; on his friendship with Bill Henderson whom this monster had destroyed, and who, please God was watching over them from wherever he was - and on his love for his lady, Cynthia, and the cornflower blue colour of her eyes.

Slowly he ceased to be aware of his surroundings, and his mind focused like a beam of hot, white light; pulsing, throwing energy along its path, boring into the creature from hell.

Time became meaningless. He might have fought for a minute, or an hour for all he knew, and yet the balance remained, neither the man from earth, or the thing from the pit giving way; each determined to win. Again and again the misshapen monster roared its anger and charged the two men, shielded only by the meagre defenses of the pentagram and the amulet; and again and again it was repulsed, thrown back by the unseen barrier of strength and light, and the air in the room became thick and fetid with the stench of its evil; and the heat increased until sweat ran in rivers down Gunn's face, soaking into his shirt. And beside him he half heard Tornquist praying, a jumble of words that had no modern meaning, and which came from another time long ago.

Gunn began to feel himself tiring, his strength draining with the continuous effort of concentration, and knew that unless he gained the edge somehow soon, he would not be able to resist much longer. And then what? What would happen to him, and Tornquist, and perhaps the rest of mankind if that awful power was let loose?

With a final effort that brought sweat again bursting to his forehead, he threw a great bolt of mental energy, coating it with light like a blue laser beam; and as the thing retreated under the onslaught, he reached into his jacket pocket with his free hand and took out a small glass bottle he had obtained in Adana. It was his last hope. If it failed he had nothing left, and it would be over.

He gripped the bottle firmly, held the amulet out again, and began to say the words of the twenty-third psalm in a loud, clear voice. As he reached the fourth verse, "Yea, though I walk through the valley of the shadow of death, I will fear no evil: for thou art with me ...", he threw the bottle, hard and straight at the stone floor beneath the creature. There was a small crack as the glass shattered.

The result was miraculous. With an ear shattering scream, the thing fell back, clawing in agony at its legs and body where the clear liquid had splashed. Again and again it roared its rage and pain and frustrated fury, and with each bellow it retreated, its form grew more indistinct, fading and losing shape, and the miasmic stench lessened. With one final effort, and for a brief second its shape hardened, and it charged the pentagram, spattering the two exhausted men with its foulness; and then, in a soundless explosion it was gone, and in the silence it left the only sound was Maxim Gunn's voice, still clear as he finished with, " ... And I will dwell in the house of the Lord forever."

Gunn slumped, exhausted. Long minutes later Tornquist recovered his voice.

`What was that?' he asked, in awed tones.

`What was what?'

`Whatever you threw at the thing.'

Gunn looked up, wiped the sweat from his eyes with his sleeve, smiling tiredly. `Holy water. I thought it might come in useful.'

`Forward planning, I suppose?'

`Sort of,' replied Gunn. `I read somewhere that the devil doesn't like it much.'

`You should do more of that kind of reading, my friend.' And Tornquist became his old ebullient self. `Now,

I think we should carry on with the rest of our plan.'

`And get out of here? I agree.' Gunn stood up, and then noticed the others in the room, still frozen like statues in a time freeze. Auntie De Lorian, ashen faced and mouth open, no longer aware of what was happening, was still trying to squeeze under the console, her thin legs twitching spasmodically. Shrinkker seemed to be dead, claimed by the heart attack that had struck him when the Thing first materialized; and the guard was still as motionless as a graven image, paralyzed with fear. `What about them?' he asked.

`What about them?' Tornquist said, shortly. `You want them as souvenirs?'

Gunn shook his head. He had a feeling that they were beyond help, and that whatever it was the Swede had in mind would make sure of that, permanently. `No,' he said. `I've had enough of them anyway. Let's go.'

The trip to the front entrance was accomplished without trouble, though there was a great deal of shouting going on in other parts of the caverns. Twice they had to slip round corners and wait, as armed guards ran past, combing the complex for them and Wanda Liszt, and Gunn had to restrain the Swede, who would rather have gone right through them, thus lowering the odds still further.

They approached the huge stone slab and found it deserted. Gunn took up position behind a convenient rock projection and cocked the machine pistol he had scooped up from the guards in the computer room, and Tornquist began a search of the walls. Presently he gave a grunt of satisfaction, and pressed on a part of it which gave way to reveal a set of concealed hieroglyphics. He studied them for a few moments, and then, turning to Gunn, said.

`Activate the opening mechanism. It's over there I think,' And he pointed to an electrical switchboard.

`Well, that certainly wasn't put in by old Gilgamesh and his pals,' said Gunn, as he went across and closed a knife switch.

There was a rumble, and the huge door slab began to move, accompanied by the whine of an electric motor. Tornquist was poised by the concealed figures.

`When I shout,' he said, `start the door closing again, and get out quickly. I don't think there'll be much time to spare.'

He turned back and pressed the figures in a certain sequence, and yelled. `Now!'

Gunn slammed the knife switch back the other way. The slab stopped, and the motor whined again as it reversed. He ducked past it and ran out into the sunshine with Tornquist hard on his heels.

`Keep going,' shouted the Swede, and bounded off across the rocks, great arms and legs pistoning. Gunn needed no urging, and followed his example, as they ran until their lungs felt like bursting; and then Tornquist threw himself down behind a large boulder, panting.

`This should do,' he gasped. `Any second ...'

Gunn felt the ground tremble under his feet, and a few small stones skittered down the cliff face. He had felt something like it in California during an earthquake, and it was eerie. And then he watched in fascination as the cliff began to tremble and shimmer out of focus as if shaken by a massive hand, and the massive stone slab of the door blew out, and was hurled across the little valley to smash against the far side. Immediately after it came a boiling explosion of dust, debris and rock, as if a huge bomb had been let off in the confines of the caverns, but there was no explosive sound, no flame, just an awe-some, almost soundless collapse. The cliff face began to crumble, and turned into a landslide of leaping boulders, crashing into the valley, and the air became thick with choking dust that almost blotted out the sun. And then, just as suddenly, it was over, and Gunn got to his feet beside Tornquist, coughing and wiping his eyes.

After a time, the dry, hot wind blew the dust cloud away, and the two men looked in awe at what had happened. A giant gash had been carved out of the cliff, and dropped in a scree slope of rubble. The result was totally unrecognizable. Utter devastation.

Gunn recovered his voice first, croaking. `What happened? That wasn't an explosion. What did you do?'

Tornquist turned to him wearily, suddenly drained of even his huge strength. `When the ancients built that place - or rather carved it out - they put in a safety device, a sort of auto-destruct button if you like. You see, they didn't want anyone to ever disturb the Great Gilgamesh, the God King, and get away with it. So they built the place like a giant pack of cards. All I did when I released those locks at the entrance was to push over one of the cards. The rest you can guess.'

`But, my God,' Gunn replied. `The Tomb, Gilgamesh, the proof, the legend; it's all gone. We could have just wrecked the computer; but now you've got nothing to show the world.'

Tornquist put his hand on Gunn's shoulder. `I think perhaps it is better this way. Some puzzles are better left unsolved. After all, Atlantis would probably be a pretty wet and gloomy place if we ever found it.'

The giant stretched his aching limbs, and then said, very firmly. `Now, let's get back to the LandRover. I haven't eaten for so long I'm beginning to forget what food looks like.'

Wanda Liszt knew she was not going to get out of the Treasure Room after all. Two things happened to tell her that. Her first emotion on seeing the creature, her alter ego, appear was fear. She had not seen it before, only communicated; but as the misty form began to materialize, she knew immediately what it was, and why it had come to her. True to the laws of black magic; having missed its target, it had come to claim her. Her dark side would take over completely, and there was no escape. And then she rose above her fear. She had known the danger; she had known the penalty of failure, and now she accepted it. There was nothing else she could do.

The second thing was an almost simultaneous deep rumble and violent shake of collapsing stone. She knew nothing of the locks that Tornquist had released, and assumed that in some way Maxim Gunn had laid an explosive charge. Again she had no fear. There had to be an end someday; and rather this way than to die of old age in a nameless bed. Her only regret was that her old enemy had finally beaten her. And yet, she managed a smile even then. Rather Maxim Gunn than anyone else. At least him she respected, and he had been a worthy enemy, neither giving nor asking quarter.

Wanda drew herself to her full height, steadying herself against the wildly shaking ground, and looked the fast materializing creature that was her other self, full in the face, her head high.

CHAPTER NINETEEN

Nothing Gunn could say would persuade Torquil Tornquist to accompany him to London to receive the thanks he deserved, and it was with genuine regret that he said good-bye and boarded his plane. As the Rolls Royce jets punched the aircraft into the clear blue sky he wondered if he had really seen the last of Wanda Liszt, and although the possibility of anyone surviving that awesome collapse was remote, Gunn knew that he would never be really satisfied until he had personally seen her lowered into the ground in a wooden box, and even then, he'd want to be the one who screwed the lid down.

He sighed and pressed the buzzer on his arm control. It was time to order a drink and think of other things.

It was late afternoon when his taxi pulled to a halt in front of the agency offices, and he got out into the mild, warm drizzle of what seemed a typical English summer. Still, on balance, he thought he preferred it to the heat and dust of Asia Minor.

He pushed through the doors at the top of the steps and was confronted by Sergeant `Earthquake' Magoon, solid as a rock, sitting in his glass-fronted cubicle.

`Afternoon, Sergeant,' he said. `Nice weather we're having.'

`Bloody typical, Sir, and welcome back.'

`Thank you. Something wrong? You don't seem your usual sunny self.'

Magoon scowled. `Disaster, Sir. Rain stopped play.'

`And I suppose we were doing well,' Gunn replied, faintly amused at his countrymen's preoccupation with sport, and cricket in particular.

`Reminded me of the old days, Sir. The Aussies might as well have gone home.'

Gunn shook his head in sympathy. `I don't have a pass, Sergeant. What's the drill?'

`That's all right, Sir,' Magoon said. `Special circumstances. I should watch out for the Chief of Staff though, he's not amused.'

`Yes,' Gunn mused. `I don't suppose he would be. This one is the decider isn't it; for the Ashes, I mean.'

`Might as well be for the fate of the world the way he's carrying on.'

`No,' Gunn smiled. `We've just taken care of that one.' And as Magoon released the lock, he walked down the corridor to the elevator.

A couple of minutes later he paused at Polly Anders' office and tossed a brightly decorated box on her desk. She glanced at it, questioningly. `For me?'

`Turkish delight,' he replied. `The genuine stuff.'

`Marvellous, but you know I have to watch my figure.'

`You eat. I'll watch,' Gunn replied, with a smile.

`The Chief wants ...' she began.

`I know,' he interrupted. `See you later.' And he went through the leather-covered door without knocking.

It was dusk when Gunn, his debriefing finished, picked up his lovely dark green Lagonda from the basement car park. The V8, 5.3 litre engine with its four Weber carburettors, rumbled into life at the touch of the key, and he surged into the rain damp evening and pointed the low, elegant nose towards his home.

He parked the car, locked it, and walked to his front steps, and as he mounted them, the front door swung open, and the ever present Sweetstory, his manservant and friend, greeted him.

`Good evening, Sir. Welcome home.'

`Thank you, Sweetstory. It's good to be here.'

`Your bath is ready, Sir, and there is a drink on the dressing table.'

`Thank you. How long do I have?'

`Half an hour, Sir. Lady Cynthia is expecting you at precisely nine o'clock.'

Gunn smiled with pleasant anticipation, and wondered, once again, just how it was that James Sweetstory always seemed to know exactly where he was. I must ask him, he thought, and mounted the stairs with long, quick strides.

And, Maxim Gunn will be back!

Was it hours, days, weeks even? Who knew. Time had no meaning under the vast mountain of tumbled rock that had been the tomb of the great king Gilgamesh. But intelligence survived, even after that holocaust, and the body it lived in moved, once, painfully, and then again, and the intelligence probed the darkness for a way out.

FUTURE TITLES TO LOOK FOR

MAXIM GUNN AND THE SLAVE WATERS

An advance group of Aliens from near the star Arcturus have chosen Britain as their base prior to a full-scale Earth invasion, as it is isolated enough by water to be contained.

Their plan. To introduce a chemical into the water supply to turn the people into zombies and slaves.

While investigating a break-in at a chemical weapons storage depot, Gunn finds evidence which makes him realize something very strange has happened.

Later he discovers the great reservoirs of Wales are the targets, with an aging ex-Nazi war criminal as the Aliens' ally. But can he stop them in time?

MAXIM GUNN AND THE SERPENT FORCE

The alignment of all nine planets will bring the Serpent Force, a mysterious power known to the Ancients, to its maximum effect in centuries. One man has the secret, and must be stopped before his insane craving for power is unleashed.

Once more Maxim Gunn is on a trail which takes him from Stonehenge to the temples of Ancient Greece and the Mayan ruins in the Yucatan.

Earthquakes, a pair of hunting panthers in a catacomb, duels with the forces of evil and unseen powers leave Gunn little time for sightseeing.

It's a race which must be won. Time is running out, and the consequences of failure are unthinkable.

MAXIM GUNN AND THE STOLEN WATERS

Was there really such a place as Atlantis? And was there a super race? Or something so different we just wouldn't want to know.

Trapped for thousands of years beneath the ocean until a submarine earthquake frees them, a few survivors emerge on a mission of revenge against the "Drylanders" whom they blame for the Great Catastrophe.

Mysterious deaths, kidnappings, blackmail and general mayhem keep Gunn fighting to stop the Atlanteans, and the world will never know how close it was.

About the Author

Nicholas Boving lives in Toronto. He was formerly a mining engineer, and as a result travelled widely in many parts of the world, which is how a lot of the Maxim Gunn backgrounds came about.

He has written several more books in the series, and looks forward to writing many more.

THE MAXIM GUNN SERIES

$7.95 Canada ($6.25 U.S.) plus $3.50 shipping & handling

Ask your bookstore to order, or
Mail Order to

TAURUS PUBLISHING
55-41 Falconer Drive, Mississauga
Ontario, Canada, L5N 1B3

E-mail: sales@tauruspub.net
Website: www.tauruspub.net

Please send me ____ copies of:

MAXIM GUNN and THE CHAOS PROJECT ______

MAXIM GUNN and THE DEMON PLAN ______

Check book or books required

I enclose $ _____ __ (money order or cheque. No COD)

Name ____

Address
____

City __________________ State/Province ________________

Zip/Post Code ______________

Prices subject to change without notice.

Please allow 4 to 6 weeks for delivery after receipt of payment.